SHE A
Savage
FOR A REAL
Gangsta
3

A NOVEL BY

VIVIAN BLUE

© 2017

Published by Royalty Publishing House

www.royaltypublishinghouse.com

ALL RIGHTS RESERVED

CHAPTER ONE

"Willow's been sleep for two days. I'm worried about her," said Cypher, frowning. "She was a mess when she arrived here, and all she had was her Gucci purse with the matching duffle bag. She collapsed into my arms, sobbing uncontrollably and didn't want to talk about what happened. All she wanted to do was take a hot shower and get some sleep, so I didn't bother her with any questions."

"You know that girl lived a dangerous life back in St. Louis," Duke pointed out. "That lil' nigga she's involved with is a serious guy. He's a fucking gangsta, and he and Willow did some shit to a good friend of mine that was unforgivable."

"What are you talking about, Duke?" Cypher continued to frown. He looked at Duke questionably because he knew something pertaining to why Willow called him frantically in the middle of the night. Duke needed to spill his fucking guts and quit beating around the bush.

"I'm not sure exactly what happened, but O'Bannon is laid up in the hospital and had to get pins and rods through his entire body. The bone in one of his legs was shattered, and his shoulder had to be popped back into the socket. Patsy said the skin on one side of his face was scraped off, and the doctors don't know if he'll be able to see out of that eye," Duke explained.

"It sounds like you're pretty bothered by this," Cypher mentioned. "But your friend O'Bannon is not my concern. It's Willow that I care about, and I'm going to make sure she's okay; even if she is fucking with JD. Maybe this is my second chance to convince her to be mine."

"Why would you want a woman who has so much baggage?" Duke questioned. "There are so many other options out there, and just the other day I ran into that model... What's her name? She's the one who came and sat on your lap the other night at the club appearance, and Indigo threw her drink in the girl's face." Cypher fired up his blunt and glared at Duke.

"I don't give a fuck about neither of them bitches! They both are two ran through hoes, trying to get at a nigga 'cause everybody's talking about me. I got the number one album in the country. I recently came off my first promotional tour, which had sold-out crowds across the country." Cypher looked at Duke smugly. "I'm that nigga, and everyone wants a piece of me. Wait until my single comes out for that new black romantic comedy. I'll be able to choose who I work with instead of the record company telling me!"

"You can write your own check, Cypher. You have made millions of dollars already, and there's so much more for the taking," Duke affirmed. "You're a big star, but soon you'll be a megastar!"

"Do you think I would be able to act in a movie?" Cypher asked curiously.

"I don't see why not. You have the one song about to come out, and I'm sure if it does well, you will be able to do an entire soundtrack like Pharrell."

"I'm not talking about that." Cypher chuckled. "I'm talking about acting. I want to be like Ice Cube. He went from being an ordinary nigga from Compton, and look at him now." Duke looked at him skeptically.

"You grew up privileged, and your mother probably could talk to someone to get you an audition for a role in something," Duke suggested.

"I want to do this on my own," Cypher professed. "She said I wouldn't be able to be a successful rapper without her and look at me! She wanted me to be a Fresh Prince type of nigga, but that didn't appeal to me. I wanted to be hardcore and fearless so that the average niggas would be able to relate to what I'm saying."

"And they do," Duke assured him. "I heard your music bumping through the streets when I went to see my wife's mother. You know she lives in Englewood, and we went down one Sunday for a barbecue. My oldest daughter said, 'Daddy, you hear Cypher's song beating in that low rider'?" Cypher's head blew up ten more notches as Duke stroked his ego like a guitar. "I think you should plan to take a trip back to New York. There were a few producers that wanted to have a meeting to discuss some projects. DJ Jam wants to put together a mixtape with you free-styling on other artists beats."

"That sounds dope, but I have to make sure that Willow's straight. I care about her and somewhat love her. I want to be with her, and this is my chance to convince her that it's the right thing to do," Cypher asserted. "She'll love all the attention that I'm going to give to her, and she'll see why staying in California is the best course of action."

"I don't know," said Duke, sounding weary. "If Willow did something to harm O'Bannon along with JD, who's to say she won't go along with JD if he opposes her staying here." Cypher hit his blunt and stared at Duke wearily. He knew the words Duke spoke could possibly be the truth. It wasn't a secret that Willow was down for JD, and when she stood in front of the nigga in his defense, that showed the power that he had over her. Cypher had to figure out how to get Willow to feel the same way about him, and being her knight in shining armor was the first step to getting what he wanted.

Willow rolled over and stared out of the large window. The curtains were slightly pulled back, and she just stared at the sky. She didn't have a clue about what day it was, or how long she'd been out of it. Her body felt slightly sore, and her stomach rumbled viciously as nausea took over. The queasy feeling made it contract violently, causing her to bring her knees up to her chest. She took a deep breath trying to keep from throwing up, but the force was much more powerful than her effort. Willow jumped up out of bed and ran urgently to the bathroom. She just barely made it to the toilet when a thick yellowish fluid projected violently out of her mouth and covered the toilet seat. She dropped to her knees, lifting the seat as she painfully dry heaved on the floor. She hadn't eaten in days, because for some reason, she had been asleep since she'd arrived. Cypher gave her a hot cup of tea, and they smoked a blunt, even though she knew she was pregnant. After that, she laid down to get some much-needed rest, and that was the last thing she remembered.

"Willow, are you all right?" asked Cypher, walking into the bathroom. He quickly made his way over to the toilet and bent down to check on her. "You've been sleep for two days, and I almost called a doctor to come check you out." He pulled her hair back as she continued to dry heave into the toilet. He felt concerned, and maybe calling a doctor would be the best course of action. He got up and walked over to the sink, grabbing one of the wash clothes that sat in a basket. She ran it under some hot water then rang it out tightly. Next, he walked over to Willow and wiped her face off. She was sitting on the floor looking worn out like she'd just come off a long drug binge, and Cypher wanted to know what the fuck was going on. "Willow, you wasn't on anything were you?" asked Cypher concerned. "I gave you a sedative to help you sleep because you were a mess when you arrived. My housekeeper said that her doctor prescribed it to her because she has trouble sleeping, so we figured it would help you to calm down. She said it was harmless, so I put it in your tea." A panicked look came across Willow's face as she lifted up her shirt and placed her hand on her stomach.

"Cypher, I'm pregnant, and I probably shouldn't have taken that. Do you think it would hurt my baby?" Willow quivered. Cypher stared at her in disbelief because he couldn't believe what he was hearing.

"You're pregnant?" Cypher stammered, letting the words process through his brain. "You're pregnant! That's wonderful!" He wrapped his arm around her neck and kissed her forehead before he placed his against hers. He hugged her tightly, even though the smell of Willow's puke was pungent. However, Cypher didn't care, because her words were like music to his ears.

"Get off of me, Cypher," Willow fussed, pushing him away. "I need some air, and this fucking puke stinks! It's nothing but stomach bile 'cause I ain't ate shit in days!" Willow wiped her mouth with her arm and got up off the floor. She looked around the bathroom while she scratched the side of her butt. It felt good to be standing up, and a hot shower was the first plan of action. "You got some 7Up or ginger ale? My stomach is upset and hurts like a muthafucka!"

"I don't know," Cypher replied. "But I can send Maria out to get some if that's what you want... and I assume that you're hungry."

"Does a hoe like dick?" Willow shot back. Cypher laughed at her response as he stood up. Even sick, Willow looked beautiful to him. Her face did look a little fatter since the last time he'd seen her, and even her nose had spread just a bit.

"I'm about to get in the shower," Willow informed him. "Can you get me some pancakes, scrambled eggs with cheese, maybe some smothered potatoes with onions and cheese, and possibly some fried chicken? A bitch is famished, and that's what I'm craving."

"You're craving shit already?" Cypher questioned and laughed. "That sounds like how you usually eat." Willow looked at him and laughed.

"That's true," Willow agreed after she thought about it. "Oh! Can I have some orange juice, and can I change my eggs to a spinach omelet with mozzarella cheese?" Cypher smiled at her.

"You can have whatever you like." Cypher beamed. "Take your shower, and I'll have Maria whip that up for you."

"Okay," Willow replied. She took off her tank top and dropped it on the floor. Cypher marveled at her naked body and couldn't wait to get in between her legs. It had been a month since they'd fucked, but he could still feel the tight warmth that captured his attention when they first had sex.

CHAPTER TWO

*J*D was up in the Ozark Mountains at his cabin. It was actually a farmhouse that his grandfather had left him when he died, and JD let his maternal uncle, Yusuf, live in it when he got out of jail. Yusuf stayed in and out of prison from the time he turned seventeen until the age of thirty. He would always come to live with his twin sister Yanni, JD's mother, and that's how her son developed a love for robbing and killing.

"Have you talked to your lady yet?" asked Yusuf, staring at his nephew, concerned.

"Naw, I ain't talked to her," JD replied sadly. "I don't know why I didn't go back to the house to get her. Shit! I should have jumped in the car with her ass. It's my job to protect her and my seed, but I was only thinking about myself in the heat of the moment. It's not like she ain't always by my side."

"Stop beating yourself up, young blood," Yusuf advised. "I think maybe she's laying low because she might have lost her phone in the shuffle of everything going on. Willow ain't no dumb girl, and I'm sure there's a logical excuse to why she's not answering the phone."

"There better be," JD fumed. "I called and left countless messages on her phone, in her DM, inbox, and email." JD looked up at his uncle with a stupid look on his face. "Who emails their gal?"

"A man who can't find his girlfriend," Yusuf answered. "Do you think that someone called the police or maybe she got pulled over and arrested?"

"Unc, I really don't know," JD sighed. "All I know is that I miss the shit out of my Lil' Baby, and I want to know whether or not she's safe."

"Did her best friend call you back? I know you say the two of them share a brain sometimes," Yusuf recalled.

"Yeah, I talked to Keena this morning, but she said that Willow hadn't called her either. She's going to reach out to this dude that might know if whether or not Willow went to California."

"Why would Willow go to California?" asked Yusuf curiously.

"Because this dude that she fucked around with lives out there. They recently were a thing, and she might have thought it was the safest place to go," JD explained. "Personally, I don't like the nigga, but it would make sense for Willow to go. At least I know that she'll be safe." JD's phone rang, and he looked down at it. "This is Keena right here. Hello."

"What's up wit' it?" Keena replied.

"Shit. Did you talk to my Lil' Baby?" asked JD, urgently.

"No, but I found out that she's in California. Charisma said Cypher picked her up from the airport early Thursday morning. He said Cypher didn't say much but mentioned that Willow was really out of it."

"Fuck!" shouted JD in frustration. "It's all my fucking fault; I shouldn't have left her! I know she's fucking furious with me, and that's why she's not answering her phone!"

"Charisma talked to Cypher this morning, and he said that Willow had been sleep since the day she'd arrived. Cypher gave her a sedative to help calm her down because she kept crying uncontrollably and couldn't stop."

"Willow's pregnant, so why the fuck is he giving her drugs?" JD fumed. "If anything happens to my seed, I swear to God I'm goin' to fuck that dude up! On my mama!"

"Calm down, JD," Keena advised. "Cypher doesn't know that Willow's pregnant, and I'm sure the drugs won't do anything to the fetus. Charisma said that he would go over to Cypher's house to tell her to call us. He figured you're probably freaking out, and I told his ass that you were cool; I guess I lied!" she laughed.

"Shut the fuck up, Keena," JD scoffed. "You know I don't play about Willow, so don't even try it!"

"I know you love my bitch, but, bruh... you ain't never wigged out like this," Keena pointed out. "We both know that Willow is insanely in love with you. She's not going to fall for any of that lame game that Cypher's going to attempt to throw at her, because her life revolves around you! Personally, I hate the nigga's guts, and if you go kill his ass, I wouldn't be sad about it. However, you have to trust Willow."

"Hold the fuck up, Keena! What did you just say?" asked JD confused. "I thought you liked Cypher." Keena got quiet and held the phone. "Uh, hello, bitch! You better say something!" Keena let out a long sigh, and JD could hear her shuffling something. "I'm waiting, Keena!"

"Okay, JD," Keena whined. "The reason why you didn't see me after all of the shit happened with Cypher and Willow in Virginia was because Cypher raped me before it all happened."

"He did what?" JD snapped. "Why the fuck didn't you say something when we were in Virginia? I would have deaded that nigga, cut his dick off, and put it in his mouth!"

"That's exactly why I didn't tell you," Keena replied. "Charisma found me battered and bruised in his tent after it happened. He wanted me to go to the hospital and report it, but I didn't want the hassle."

"You didn't want the hassle? Are you stupid or something, Keena!" JD yelled. "It wouldn't have been a hassle to at least whoop that nigga's ass! And I bet you didn't tell Willow because she would have shot his ass instead of loading up ole boy." Yusuf looked at JD strangely before he walked back into the house.

"Please, don't tell Willow, JD. I'm begging you!" Keena pleaded. "I want to be the one to tell her, and right now isn't the time for it. I want to wait until she's made it back home. Right now, there is so much uncertainty."

"You're telling me! I don't even know if the nigga, O'Bannon, is still alive or not. KC and Stan drove back to St. Louis this morning, and they're supposed to call me with a report once they do a sweep," JD explained. "I told Willow to get some money to take with her, so she should be straight. I'm truly fuckin' kickin' myself because I should have gone back to the house to get her."

"Yes, you should have, but I'm sure Willow understands why you kept going," Keena assured him. "If don't nobody else know you, JD, Willow has your uglass pegged." Both Keena and JD laughed.

"I hope she does understand," JD agonized. "You know she's a real bitch when she's mad at me, and I can hear her mouth right now complaining about me leaving her." They held the phone in silence for several minutes.

"Well, JD, I'm about to get off this phone. My grandmother is taking me shopping because she said I dress like a cheap whore," Keena chuckled. "I can't believe she says the whole word. Most black people say hoe or ho, but not my grandmother. She says, 'whore'!" JD laughed at Keena because he knew she was trying to lighten the mood. "Stop blaming yourself, and wait for her to call you, JD. Even if she is mad at you, she'll eventually come around. She can only stay mad at your for like a day or so." Keena laughed.

"Fuck you, Keena! Get off my phone," JD ordered. "I love you."

"I love yo' funky ass too. Bye!" Keena hung up the phone, and JD just stared out at the beautiful scenery. All he wanted to do was hear his beloved's voice through the telephone, and he would be able to calm down. She saved his life, and there was no way he could ever repay her, but he made a promise to himself to always protect her, and make sure that she's always happy.

"Nephew, did you locate her?" asked Yusuf, coming out on the porch.

"Kind of," JD replied, looking up at his uncle. "Keena located her, and she is in California with that nigga, but…" JD drifted off, thinking about what Keena told him.

"But what?" asked Yusuf, clueless. JD stood from the wooden steps of the porch.

"Keena just told me that the bitch ass nigga, Cypher, raped her when we were at a festival in Virginia," JD disclosed.

"Damn!"

"I know, right," JD blurted out. "But that ain't the problem. Keena doesn't want me to tell Willow, but I don't hide shit from her, and that's the one thing we promised each other the day I asked her to marry me. We both agreed to never hide anything or keep secrets from one another. Also, we said we would never go to bed angry at one another, but I bet her ass is fuming right now." JD put his hands on top of his head and let out a deep breath.

"It's almost prayer time," Yusuf announced. "I think you should come inside and pray with me." JD didn't say anything. "Have you been praying, nephew? You know it's the only way to stay balanced in this crazy world. Do you remember how to do it?"

"Yeah, I remember," JD replied, frowning.

"Good," said Yusuf. "I'll go get the prayer mats."

CHAPTER THREE

*W*illow walked back into the bedroom and lay across the bed. She had thrown up all of the food that Maria had prepared for her and some extra stomach acid that felt the need to be released. She was frustrated that nothing seemed to be staying down, and Cypher was taking a long time to come back from the store with her soda. There was nothing like being in the hood because all they had to do is go up the street. Cypher lived somewhere in Santa Monica, and going to the store wasn't the same as going in St. Louis.

Willow noticed her phone sitting on the nightstand, and she wondered if she had any charge left in her battery. She grabbed it and attempted to turn it on, but it was dead. She reached over, grabbed her purse, and took the charger out of it. She plugged it into the wall then into her phone with the dread of seeing a million missed calls from JD. She was a bit pissed at him for not coming to get her, because he knew that she would be a basket case without him during a time of panic. He did almost die, so self-preservation was the key to survival at that time.

Willow powered up her phone and waited for a few minutes. Just as she suspected, there were at least a hundred voice messages, about fifty text messages, and Lord knows how many DMs. Also, she had a few emails that struck her as strange. Willow knew it was mostly JD, so she took the time to listen, read, and take in all of the information, cussing, and fussing that he did on each one. She knew her man loved her, so it was cute that he was raising such a fuss.

Willow pulled her hair back with a ponytail holder and washed her face. She wanted to look rested when she FaceTimed JD because she didn't want to hear his mouth about her appearance. She smoothed some cocoa butter on her face then applied a little Vaseline so her lips didn't look dry and chapped. Next, she walked back into the room and climbed onto the bed, ready to see her Big Baby. The tank top she had on clung to her breasts, and you could see the entire outline of her areolas. She figured JD would get a rise out of it, but then she wondered if he would be pissed off when he found out she was staying with Cypher. He was the only person she could think of that was far enough away from St. Louis to be considered safe, and if JD had something to say about it, she would point out the fact that he left her in a frantic state with no plans of coming to get her. Willow was pissed at JD for his inconsideration, but she knew he was under a lot of pressure, and getting away was his top priority in the heat of the moment.

Willow grabbed her phone and selected JD's number. She pressed the button to FaceTime with him and waited patiently for him to answer. Her stomach was churning due to nervousness and nausea. There wasn't shit left in her stomach to come out, so she couldn't figure out for the life of her why she felt sick.

"What the fuck, Lil' Baby! I haven't talked to your ass in two fuckin' days, and I was going crazy!" JD snapped, staring at her sternly.

"Hi, JD. How are you?" said Willow sarcastically. "I'm fine, and it's refreshing to know that now you give a fuck about me after you kept going and didn't come to get me from the house!" The grimace on her face matched the one he was wearing, and his face softened when he picked up on her expression.

"I was worried about you, Willow, and I realized I fucked up when I didn't turn back around to get you," JD confessed. "How you feeling, baby mama?"

"Do you really fucking care, JD? You left me at the apartment like I didn't mean shit to you! I was alone, afraid, and didn't know what to do!"

"I miss you, baby, and I want to apologize for leaving you hanging. My mind was all over the place, and all I could think about was getting the fuck away. I should have jumped in the car with you, and we could have gone to the house then headed to the Ozarks. I assumed you would have remembered, but that's my fault for not reminding you," he acknowledged.

"You know I have an attitude with you, right?" Willow snapped.

"I know, Lil' Baby, and I'll take it this time," JD replied smugly. "Pull that phone back some so I can take a look at you. You ain't gave up any of my pussy, have you?" Willow frowned angrily at JD because she couldn't believe he said some shit like that to her.

"Who the fuck you talkin' to?" she snapped. "Why would you assume that I would do something like that? My pussy belongs to you, so ain't no other nigga gone be running up in these walls! You just better make sure that you don't stick your dick in nothing but your pants, or I'll be wearing that muthafucka as a medallion on my Cuban link!"

"Damn! Who's that going off like that?" asked Yusuf, stepping out on the porch.

"This is Willow's crazy ass wigging out on me for nothing," JD replied.

"Who the fuck are you tellin' that you're talking to me?" spat Willow full of attitude.

"You betta calm the fuck down, Willow, for real before I be on the next plane to Cali to get in that ass!" JD barked.

"Well, come the fuck on, JD, 'cause you know I ain't scared!" she shot back. She pulled the phone back some, and he noticed her erect nipples. A sudden sadness came across JD. He wanted to be laying on his pillows and smelling her sweet scent.

"Tell me you love me," JD demanded. Willow lifted an eyebrow as her lips remained tuned up. "Tell me you love me, man!"

"I'm not telling you that right now, 'cause I'm fucking mad at you! You fucking left me, and now I'm forced to deal with this sappy ass nigga who thinks that we should be together." She huffed. "You get on my fuckin' nerves, man! You think that telling me that you love me is going to make everything okay, but it's not!"

"So the fuck what! You just better make sure that nigga don't lay a finger on you!" JD insisted. "'Cause I'm not beyond puttin' a plug in that nigga's ass, and this will be the first time that I beat yo' ass!" Normally, Willow got a kick out of JD talking to her like this, but today was not the day for yanking her chain.

"You mad or nah, JD?" Willow snapped. "'Cause if you're mad, you know I don't give a fuck! I'm so pissed off at you right now, and normally, the shit that you do doesn't piss me off, but this just ain't that day!"

"What?" JD replied. "But yo' ass gone care when I appear at that nigga's doorstep to get you!"

"Yo' weak ass ain't gone do shit! You don't even know where the fuck I'm at to come and get me wit' yo' inconsiderate ass!"

"Yo' ass is starting to really piss me off, Lil' Baby, so you better check yo' self and yo' smart ass mouth 'cause I ain't in the mood for this shit! I miss the fuck out of you right now, so chill the fuck out!" Willow was fuming. Even though she missed him terribly, she couldn't get over the fact that he left her.

"You think this is a joke, JD? 'Cause I sure as fuck ain't laughing! I'm fucking serious when I say that I'm mad at you, and it's going to be a minute before I get over the shit!"

JD wasn't trying to hear none of the shit Willow was saying. She couldn't be mad at him, because he was the man of the relationship, and she had to understand that sometimes a nigga fucks up.

"Pull up your shirt, and let me see them pretty titties," JD instructed with a bit of authority.

"Fuck naw," Willow replied defiantly. "I ain't showing you shit! How about you think about and remember what these muthafuckas looked like the last time you saw them 'cause it's probably going to be a while before you see these bitches again!" She hung up the phone and threw it on the bed. Her hormones had her attitude raging, and she didn't want to be bothered with JD's insensitive ass. She was going to make his ass suffer through whatever emotional stress that he was going through right now.

JD was pissed off that Willow had hung up on him. He felt that what he had done was an honest mistake, and he couldn't believe that Willow was acting this way. He missed his girlfriend like a muthafucka, which meant that he probably wasn't going to get a wink of sleep tonight. He hated Willow being mad at him, and somehow, he was going to have to make it right.

CHAPTER FOUR

O'Bannon was laid up in the hospital bed, pissed that he couldn't get up and walk. He shattered the bones in his left leg and dislocated his hip when he landed from being hit by a car. He was unconscious for a few minutes and didn't come around until Ricky ran over to check on him. They weren't expecting for JD to be ready for an ambush, and JD and his crew totally outgunned the four men.

"How you feeling?" asked Patsy, walking into the hospital room. "The doctors said you were very lucky to only injure one side of your body."

"I'm in so much pain." O'Bannon grimaced. "The side of my face feels like it's on fire."

"That's because all of the skin is gone," Patsy explained. "The doctors are going to do a skin graft and use the skin from the inside and back of your thighs and butt to replace the missing skin on your face, neck, and arm." O'Bannon laid silent for a few minutes because he was still a bit groggy from the medicine. They had him heavily sedated to help him cope with the excruciating pain that he was experiencing. "You got fucked up bad, O, but what I want to know is why were you out at the Chain of Rocks Bridge when you were supposed to be at The

Olive Bar promoting the event?"

"I was handling some business." O'Bannon grimaced. "How did I end up at the hospital anyway?"

"Ricky called the ambulance to come pick your ass up. He said something about you getting hit by a black Dodge Challenger, and that's it. He said you were knocked up in the air and came down on your side. That's why you're just fucked up on the left side."

"Tell Ricky to come up here and talk to me. I need to know what happened," O'Bannon replied.

"You never answered my question, O'Bannon. Who was the person that hit you with the car, and why were you—"

"Shut the fuck up, Patsy! If you can't stand here and be quiet, then get the fuck out!" O'Bannon grimaced. He rolled his head over to the side because he was pissed off. He had JD right where he wanted him and was about to dome his ass when he was hit by the car. He didn't see Willow in the truck they were in, and that was unusual because JD always had Willow with him when handling business. O'Bannon wondered was she the one who hit him with the car. If she was, he had every intention on getting her ass locked up! Shit was getting out of control when it came to the situation with Willow. He thought she would be more loyal to him, but it seemed that, for some reason, JD had more influence, and that definitely was the problem.

****

Charisma had a problem that needed to be dealt with urgently. He managed to hire a lawyer to represent Casey Bridges, the man arrested for attempted first-degree robbery and armed criminal action against

Cypher, but he hadn't been released yet. The police did a nationwide police check and found that he was wanted in two other states for the same offenses. He had been calling Charisma, threatening to tell the police the truth about how he was hired by Charisma to rob Cypher. He demanded that Charisma find out how much it would cost to get his lawyer to clear these charges, or Charisma was going to be in a jail cell next to him. Charisma was freaking out because he knew he wouldn't make it in prison. Also, a lot had been happening with him. The same record label that Cypher was signed to was looking to ink a deal with him.

Charisma knew his criminal cousins had a lot of connections throughout the country, and he was the one who hooked Charisma up with Casey. His oldest cousin, Ronnie, had spent ten years in the Feds, so he met a lot of people that he kept in contact with in case there was something he needed them for. Ronnie's little brother Jay was a stone-cold gangbanger that lived by the code of the street. He represented Crips hard, and the tattoos on his body were a walking billboard that let anyone who saw him know what set he was claiming. Charisma needed to speak with Ronnie because he wanted to see if Ronnie had someone up in Virginia that could take care of his problem. The record company had promised to pay him a signing bonus once they had a contract worked out, and he could use the money to pay for Ronnie's help.

"What's up, Ronnie?" said Charisma, hyped.

"Aye! What's up, cuzzo?" asked Ronnie enthusiastically. "When yo' ass get back in town?"

"That nigga's been back in town for a minute, but I guess he thinks he's too good to come see us," spat his little cousin Jay.

"Ah, nigga, it ain't nothing like that." Charisma tried to laugh it off. "I had to hit the studio as soon as I got back because me and that nigga Cypher had to lay down a track for a movie that's coming out next year."

"More like Cypher got a song, and yo' ass gone be in the background making sounds," Jay replied sarcastically and laughed. "I thought you said that you was gone be rapping on that nigga's album. I downloaded it, and I ain't hear shit from you but a bunch of ad-libs."

"See, what had happened was all the producers were hatin' on me," Charisma tried to explain. "I had verses on a few tracks, but they told Cypher with it being his first album, he should only have known rappers on his shit."

"Ah," Jay replied. "You gone be on the new album he's working on? And when is he gon' set that new crib out and have a dope ass house party?"

"Now, that I don't know," Charisma replied. "He got some chick staying there with him right now, and she probably ain't having that shit."

"I thought Cypher was fucking with Indigo," Ronnie mentioned. "That lil' bitch is fine as hell! I'd like to get real familiar with that fat ass of hers!" Charisma looked at him funny because he'd been sneaking around with Indigo for a few months. They started fooling around while on tour, and when they got back to California, they continued to mess around. She really wasn't fucking Charisma. Sucking dick was her act of choice because she felt like to give up that much pussy would totally wear her shit out. Charisma was fortunate enough to spend nights with her off and on when she didn't find some other victim to pounce on, and that's when he would get to fuck. Charisma was sure that he would be able to convince Indigo that he was the best choice for her, but until then, he would take it how it comes.

"Naw, she ain't jammin' with Cypher like that for real. They're just doing it for appearances, and like I said, Cypher has a new bitch that he's been courting."

"Ah, yeah! Is she famous?" asked Ronnie curiously.

"Nope, but you'd like her, Ronnie. She's from St. Louis and a real gangsta bitch!" Charisma smiled.

"Oh yeah," Ronnie sang. "If she's a gangsta, what the fuck she wants with Cypher?"

"I don't know. I asked the same question." Charisma laughed. "Can I holla at you about something in private?"

"Sure, cuzzo. Let's go into the house to talk," Ronnie suggested.

"Okay," Charisma replied, feeling a bit nervous. They walked into Ronnie's house and went back to the kitchen. Ronnie's wife was preparing lunch for him, and she smiled when Charisma walked through the door.

"Charisma!" she shouted and smiled. "Where have you been?"

"Hi, Lisa," he replied, returning the smile. "You're looking good and pregnant." She smiled and rubbed her belly.

"This one is due in two months, and I can't wait!" She beamed.

"How is Cypher, and when are you guys going to have a big party so we can come kick it!"

"You don't look like you're in any shape to kick it." Charisma laughed.

"Boy, don't let this belly fool you! I still goes out and kicks it!" Lisa frowned. "You know Ronnie ain't gone let nobody bump me or shit."

"No doubt," Charisma agreed. "Where are the other kids?"

"Everybody's at school, and Lil' Ronnie is with my mama at the store," Lisa explained. "You know he'll be three next month."

"Damn, it doesn't seem like the lil' nigga should be that old. I remember when you went in labor with him." Charisma smiled warmly at Lisa because he really loved talking with her.

"Come on and have a seat, nigga, so we can talk," Ronnie offered. "You hungry?"

"I really don't have time, 'cause I got to get across town to meet Cypher, but I really need to ask you for a favor," Charisma explained.

"What's up?" asked Ronnie curiously.

"I got this problem, and I need your assistance with it," said Charisma nervously.

"You need me to kill someone?" asked Ronnie, directly.

"Not exactly, but death might be the end game," Charisma explained. "I hired that guy to rob Cypher and rough him up to prove that his ass ain't really as gangsta as he portrays, but the shit went bad."

"What do you mean?" Ronnie asked, interested in Charisma's

conversation. Charisma looked over at Lisa who didn't seem to be paying any attention to their conversation.

"From what I understand, dude had Cypher hemmed up against his tour bus, ready to fuck him up and take his shit. Well, the chick that Cypher's fucking with was on the bus and came out to stop him. Dude said Willow wasn't afraid of him, and she shot him when he refused to back down or walk away."

"That sounds like my type of woman," Jay chimed in, walking into the kitchen. Charisma looked back at Jay then turned back around to face Ronnie.

"Anyway, in case you forgot ole boy's name, it's Casey Bridges, and he's being held in Virginia. I paid his bond to get him released, but apparently, he had two other warrants in other states. He's threatening to rat on me if I don't pay the charges for his other warrants." Charisma frowned. "Do you think you can reach out to some of your contacts to get him taken care of?"

"We need to talk a little more in-depth about some shit before I can say whether or not I can help you. Where are you meeting up with Cypher?" asked Ronnie.

"Huh? I'm meeting him at the studio in downtown L.A.," Charisma replied. "Why?"

"Nigga, don't question me," Ronnie snapped. "Just write the address down." Charisma looked at him stupidly and grabbed the pen off the table to write the address down. He wasn't sure why Ronnie wanted to know it, but suddenly, he felt like maybe this wasn't a good idea.

CHAPTER FIVE

*W*illow was standing in front of a large dressing mirror studying herself. She wanted to see if there were any noticeable differences with her face or her body since she found out that she was pregnant. She gathered the hem of the shirt she was wearing and pulled it up, exposing her stomach. Cypher walked into the room and smiled when he noticed what she was doing. He was excited about her being pregnant and couldn't wait to discuss her moving to California permanently to live with him.

"What are you in here doing?" Cypher asked, walking up on Willow. He wrapped his arms around her waist and rubbed his hands across her belly.

"What are you doing?" asked Willow defensively. She moved away from Cypher and looked at him strangely.

"Why did you move away from me like that?" Cypher asked, confused. He grabbed Willow's hand and tried to pull her to him, but she pulled it away. "Wait a fuckin' minute, Willow! What the fuck is going on? You called me frantically and said you needed my help. I picked you up from the airport with no questions asked, and you were a bumbling mess! You tell me that you're pregnant, and now you're pulling away from me like I've done something wrong." Willow stared at him unconcerned as she placed her hands on her hips.

"Cypher, I appreciate all of your help, but there's something we need to discuss," said Willow, sitting down on the end of the bed.

"Okay," said Cypher, walking up to her. He kneeled down and wrapped his arms around her waist. Willow gave him an uncomfortable look, but Cypher ignored it. He figured she might still be mad at him for what happened in Virginia, but they had talked since then, and it seemed like all was forgiven. "What's up, baby mama? What seems to be the problem?"

"That's the problem." Willow huffed. "You're not my baby's daddy, so I don't feel comfortable with you touching all on me like that." Cypher's face went from pleasant to angry instantly.

"What the fuck you mean? You said that shit to me before, and I just thought you were being moody like pregnant women tend to be!" he snapped. "I was all up in those guts when we were together. How you figure that I'm not the father of your baby?"

"Because I'm only five weeks pregnant, so I couldn't possibly be pregnant by you," Willow explained. "I'm engaged to be married to JD, and it's very disrespectful to have you groping all on me inappropriately."

"I think you're lying, Willow," Cypher complained. "Are you still mad at me about what happened in Virginia? I was heavily under the influence of drugs and alcohol, so that's why I was being a total asshole."

"Virginia doesn't have shit to do with anything, Cypher. I'm with JD now, and I'm loyal to him." Willow frowned. "I knew it was a mistake coming here when I boarded the plane. I knew you were going to take my visit out of context and—"

"Why the fuck did you come here, Willow?" Cypher snapped. "I thought that the nigga might have beat yo' ass or something, and you were running out here to get away from him. You know I care about you, Willow, and you can tell JD that you lied about the baby being his."

"You've must have lost your fuckin' mind!" Willow shouted, jumping up from the bed. The force from her standing made Cypher fall back on the floor, and Willow stepped over him to get away. "There's no way in hell I'm going to lie about some shit like that! This is JD's baby, and I ain't gone lie for nobody!" Willow pulled out her phone and texted Shaggy.

Willow: *Hey Hun! Cypher is being a bitch, so can I come crash with you for about a week or so?*

"So, humor me, Willow," said Cypher, getting up off the floor. "What happened that your ass is here in California with me?" Willow stared at him in frustration because what she really needed was a friend right now.

"Cypher, I'm sorry if you felt like I was coming here to be with you. It might have been selfish of me to impose my problems on you."

"Willow, tell me why you're here, and stop beating around the bush!" snapped Cypher. "I don't have time to be playin' games with you, and I'll throw your ass out if you don't start leveling with me!" Willow stared at Cypher angrily because she couldn't believe the nigga was threatening her. She had her cell phone in her pocket, and it dinged while Cypher was fussing at her. She pulled it out and saw that it was Shaggy responding to her text message.

31

Shaggy: *You're in town! Shit yeah, you can stay as long as you like! Where are you, now?* A smirk came across her face as she sent Shaggy another message.

Willow: *I'm at Cypher's house. Can you come get me, now?"*

"Who the fuck are you texting?" snapped Cypher, reaching for Willow's phone. She turned her body away from him to the side, and he grabbed her by the waist trying to get it. Willow elbowed him across the jaw by accident, and Cypher stared at her angrily. Willow's mouth dropped open when she saw a bit of blood on his lip because he bit down on it by accident. He put his hand up to his mouth and touched it then pulled it away and stared at the blood.

"I'm sorry, Cypher," Willow stammered. "I didn't mean to elbow you. Let me take a look."

"You've done enough," Cypher frowned. Willow softened her face, and Cypher saw the sincerity in her eyes.

"I'm really sorry, Cypher. Let me take a look." Cypher moved his hand and let Willow take a look. She narrowed her eyes and saw where his teeth had cut his lip. "You'll be alright."

"No, I won't," Cypher scoffed and frowned. "I can't believe you're playing me like this, Willow. I love you!"

"You haven't known me long enough to love me, Cypher," Willow replied frankly. "You love my doggy style and tight pussy." Cypher thought for a second.

"Yeah, I love those things too, but that's not what I'm talking about. Willow, I love you! I think about you every second of the day. When I roll over in the bed, I tend to reach for you. I hear your voice when I'm lost in my thoughts, and I just want to hold you in my arms and never let you go!" Willow looked at Cypher in shock. She didn't realize that Cypher had such caring feelings for her.

"I'm sorry, Cypher, but I don't feel the same way about you," Willow confessed. "Again, I care for you, but I'm not in love with you. I love JD with all my heart and soul, and I can't see myself with anyone except him." A mean scowl came across Cypher's face again. He reached out and grabbed Willow firmly by the arms.

"Where the fuck is JD now, huh?" Cypher spat angrily. "I don't see that muthafucka here with you making sure you're okay. Why did you have to run to California to me, huh?" Willow stared at him vehemently because she couldn't believe the muthafucka grabbed her so aggressively.

"It's none of your fuckin' business where JD is," Willow shot back. "It was a fucking mistake coming here with you, but don't worry about it, 'cause I'm about to get the fuck up out of here!" She tried to break away from Cypher, but he had a strong hold on her arms. She looked from side to side then back up at him. He must have lost his mind if he thought he was going to manhandle her.

"You better take your hands off of me, Cypher, or you're going to be sorry," Willow advised him. Cypher looked at her with a lifted eyebrow and laughed.

"You ain't gone do shit!" Cypher shot back. The look on Willow's face turned even angrier, and for some reason, Cypher got a rise out of it. "You gon' shut the fuck up and be more cooperative, bitch!" Cypher pressed his lips firmly against Willow's, and her eyes widened in shock. He slid his tongue inside of Willow's mouth, and it utterly disgusted her and pissed her off even further!

Willow bit down on Cypher's tongue hard and kneed him in the nuts. Cypher tried to yell out in pain, but Willow still had her teeth dug down on his tongue. She pushed him hard against his shoulders, and Cypher fell to the floor.

"You bitch!" Cypher shouted as he rolled around on the floor holding his dick and balls. "I'm goin' to fuck you up!"

"Aaaaaaaaaa… not if you can't catch me!" Willow replied, laughing. She ran over to the bed and grabbed her phone charger off of it. Next, she ran around to the other side and gathered her clothes up off the floor. Cypher was still rolling around in pain because she kneed him real good in the groin.

"Bitch, when I catch you, I swear to God I'm fucking you up!" Cypher howled. Willow shoved all of her stuff in her bag and went into the bathroom to get her toothbrush and other toiletries, but when she came back out, Cypher was on his feet and staring at her angrily. "Bitch, you gone learn that I ain't the muthafucka to be played with! I'm gone teach your ungrateful ass a lesson, and you gone learn to love me!"

"Your ass is delusional, and if you know what's best for you, Cypher, you'll get the fuck out of my way!"

"What you gon' do?" Cypher asked arrogantly. "You don't have a gun like you did in Virginia when you shot that dude. How would you like it if I tell the police that I lied for you, and the man who attacked me was unarmed and begging for his life when you shot him!"

"You can call and tell them muthafuckas whatever you want!"

Willow shot back. "It ain't like I've never been arrested for attempted murder, so do what the fuck you feel is necessary, bitch ass nigga!" Cypher narrowed his eyes at her, and his knees bent inward cause his nuts were in excruciating pain. "If you know what's best for you, you'll get the fuck out of my way and let me leave. JD won't take kindly to the threats you've made against me, and he'll fly straight out to California to kill yo' ass! As a matter of fact, let me FaceTime him right now!" Willow went to pull her phone out of her pocket, and Cypher rushed her. He tackled her to the floor, and Willow's phone flew out of her hand and slid across the floor.

"I don't know where we went wrong," Cypher whispered. "You were once in love with me, and you can't deny it!" He managed to pin Willow's hands against the floor, and he stared down at her angrily. However, when he saw the despair on her face, it triggered something inside of him, and his angry scowl instantly turned to remorse. "What am I doing?"

"That's what I was about to ask," Shaggy declared, standing in the doorway. "Get the fuck up off of her right now!" Cypher turned to see Shaggy standing behind him. "You better get the fuck up off of Willow, or the both of us are going to beat yo' ass!"

"That's right!" Willow shouted. Cypher hesitated for a second but knew better than to challenge the both of them. He slowly got up off the floor and held his hand out to help Willow up. She stared at him, grimacing so he decided to take his hand anyway.

"I'm sorry, Willow," Cypher apologized. "I really am in love with you, and I just can't understand why you don't want to love me back."

Willow stared at him with a frown still on her face. She empathized with him because she understood how he felt, but it didn't excuse the fact that he attacked her.

"No hard feelings," Willow replied, then she sucker punched him in the jaw and followed up with a jab in the gut. "But, you done fucked up!" She walked around him and grabbed her bag to leave with Shaggy. Cypher had his arm across his stomach and one hand on his jaw; not to mention, his nuts were still aching. Willow didn't hit like a girl, and that completely threw Cypher off. He figured because Willow was pregnant, she would be less resistant. However, he was sadly mistaken, and Willow completely fucked him up!

CHAPTER SIX

"*N*ephew, we need to go make this move," said Yusuf, moving quickly through the living room.

"What kind of move?" JD asked with a bit of an attitude. "I'm not on a working vacation. I'm trying to lay low because the police might be looking for me."

"Ain't no police looking for you," Yusuf assured him. "I called a few of my contacts in St. Louis, and they said ain't no report or warrant been issued for you nor Willow."

"That don't mean shit to me! I know O'Bannon, and he's probably got a few guys out there looking for me," JD fussed. "Besides, why every time I come down to this muthafucka, you got some job for me?" JD was really pissed off because Willow had hung up on him. He tried to call her back to go off, but she refused to answer the phone.

"You don't even know what the fuck I'm talking about," Yusuf replied and smiled. "I bet you assume that it's something scandalous."

"I ain't assuming shit!" JD shot back. "Willow has taught me to never assume anything 'cause you ain't gone make an ass out of me!" Yusuf laughed at his nephew. There was a time when Yusuf would tell JD to come go with him, and JD would jump up with no hesitation.

"You getting soft on me, nephew?" Yusuf asked jokingly. JD glared up at him and bit his bottom lip.

"Ain't shit soft on me but my dick, and that's because my bitch ain't around," JD scoffed. "Now gone, Unc, before I say something, and we be out here bangin'."

"You'd swing on me, JD?" Yusuf asked, surprised.

"Do a crackhead love crack?" JD shot back. Yusuf's brow furrowed as he thought about the situation at hand.

"What have I done to you, JD, for you to come at me disrespectfully like this?" Yusuf complained. "All I've ever done was tried to teach you how to survive in this world that don't love you! I've taught you to have a relationship with God, be loving and respectful to your mother, and how to get down how you live in these streets. The way I see it, you owe me everything, but all I ask for is respect!"

"Nigga, fuck you!" JD scoffed, jumping to his feet. "Yeah, you taught me a lot, and I thank you for that, but, nigga, you ain't my daddy. And if my memory serves me correctly, you got my mama turned out on crack, and I did a two-year stretch in juvenile because of yo' ass! So, don't try to get all sanctimonious and shit on me or try to make it seem like you've been my savior!"

"Damn, lil' nigga, it sounds like you got some animosity toward me or something." Yusuf chuckled. "Tell me how you really feel."

"You don't want me to do that, bruh," JD uttered and laughed. "'Cause I guarantee an ass whoopin' goin' to follow!"

"Oh! You think I'm going to whoop your ass after you express yourself to me?" Yusuf asked, amused. JD looked at his uncle smugly and turned up his lips.

"Naw, nigga! I'm gon' whoop yo' ass, and it's goin' to cause you to feel some type of way and try to jump sharp with me. That's when I'm gon' show you what you won, and you don't want that smoke!" JD assured him. His phone started going off in his pocket, but he ignored it because it was important that he and his uncle finish their conversation. JD loved his uncle unconditionally, but he still harbored some ill feelings toward him. The police were always beating at their door looking for Yusuf, and one time, the police roughed up his mother because they couldn't find Yusuf.

"Nigga, I ain't the reason why Yanni was strung out on dope! You need to ask yo' daddy about that shit!" Yusuf shot back. "Yeah, I introduced her to crack, but that nigga was giving it to her! He would drop off large quantities of it—"

"For her to put up and hide until he got back! You know if I would have told my daddy you tried to blame him for my mama being a dope fiend, he'd come straight here and murk yo' bitch ass!" JD spat angrily. He frowned at his uncle because that nigga must have lost his mind! "I don't believe you even tried to come at me with that bogus ass shit!"

"Nigga, what!" Yusuf scoffed. "Yo' mama is my twin sister, and I love her with all of my heart! When was the last time you've seen her?" JD mugged his uncle because it had been at least three years since he'd seen her. "I can't hear you!" said Yusuf, putting his hand up to his ear. "Exactly! You don't even know where yo' mama is, do you?"

JD rolled his eyes angrily because he didn't feel like continuing the conversation. He felt like his mother really didn't love him because she had put him through so much as a child. Granny was the only person that he felt loved him, and his relationship with Sam didn't develop until JD got older.

"I'm done talking about this shit," JD declared. "I ain't goin' nowhere with you, and if you want to go knock off some store or drug farm, then you're on your own. I'm just trying to buy my time until I can get to my bitch and baby!" Yusuf looked at JD with pity. He knew that JD's life was rougher than the average kid, but he knew his nephew was full of hurt and pain.

"Have it your way, nephew, but I want you to know that I still love you! You can hate me, have ill intent toward me for things that I've done to you in the past, but I've made amends with God about it, and I hope that you'll be able to forgive me someday," Yusuf offered humbly. He walked passed JD and went to get in the truck. "I was going to go take you to see someone, but I guess now is not the time." Yusuf got into his truck and started it up. He let the window down and stared at his nephew admirably. "You're one tough lil' nigga, but one day all that tough shit is going to be your demise." Yusuf drove off, leaving JD to ponder his words. All JD ever had in this world was his strength, and that's what got him through those even tougher times.

Yusuf drove down the road contemplating an impromptu meeting between JD and Yanni. She had come to the Ozarks almost a year ago, and Yusuf convinced her to check into a rehab facility. She worked the program and decided to move into a home with other recovering addicts that was run by a group of nuns. A part of her rehabilitation was making amends with the people she'd hurt the most during her time of addiction. This was very difficult for Yanni because there was so much hurt, pain, and regret that she felt toward JD for various reasons. She blamed him for a lot of stuff that wasn't his fault, but because he was there, he was the person that she took all of her anger and frustration out on. Yusuf wanted to bring JD along on his visit because he felt that it would do both of them some good. Yusuf knew that Yanni would be excited about being a grandmother, and he wanted both Yanni and JD to heal in order to grow close like they once were.

Yusuf pulled up at the gates of the farm and sat there for a second contemplating his words. He wanted to tell Yanni that JD was in town, but he didn't want to upset her or put any pressure on her that would trigger a relapse. They had done an exercise in group one day, and it upset Yanni so much that she showed up on Yusuf's porch drunk as a skunk. She had to go back to the rehab facility for thirty more days and start the process all over.

"Are you going to sit at the gate or go on down?" asked Sister Sarah. Yusuf snapped out of his thoughts and looked at her. He smiled brightly at her because he was quite fond of her beauty.

"I was actually hoping that I would see your beautiful face, Sister Sarah." Yusuf smiled. "It always brightens my day when I see your lovely smile."

"Ah, Yusuf! Your sister said you were a charmer," Sister Sarah replied with a big smile on her face. "Are you here to see Yanni? I know she'll be happy to see you."

"Yes, I am," Yusuf replied. "Can I give you a lift down to the house?"

"Only if you promise to talk dirty to me," Sister Sarah joked. Yusuf's eyes widened, and Sister Sarah fell out laughing. "I'm just joking, Yusuf. I would love a ride."

"Okay, Sister Sarah." Yusuf laughed. "I'll talk dirty to you and follow up with a little…" Yusuf caught himself. "You don't want these problems, Sister Sarah." She looked at him and smiled.

"You don't know what I want," Sister Sarah replied, opening the door. "I wasn't always a good sister."

"I bet you were something else!" Yusuf added.

"Man! I could tell you some stories." They both laughed as Yusuf drove them to the house. They continued to laugh and flirt back and forth. It was something that Yusuf always looked forward to.

"I'm starting to think that you come to visit Sister Sarah instead of me," said Yanni, walking up to the truck.

"If Sister Sarah doesn't stop flirting with me, I'm gonna grab her booty!" Yusuf mentioned intently. Sister Sarah looked back at Yusuf as she got out of the truck.

"Don't be surprised if I grab yours back," Sister Sarah shot back. Then, she looked at Yusuf and winked. "Hi, Yanni."

"Hi, Sister Sarah," Yanni replied, laughing. "Is Yusuf harassing you?"

"Not at all." Sister Sarah smiled. "Yusuf better watch himself, though." She smiled, bit her bottom lip, and walked off toward the house.

"Ouuu, Yusuf." Yanni laughed. "You hear what Sister Sarah told you?" Yusuf gave a toothy grin and laughed.

"Sister Sarah better watch herself! I'll catch that ass out in the field and make her ass see both Jesus and Moses while I'm parting that Red Sea!" Yanni laughed heartily. "I've got some news for you."

"Really?" asked Yanni cheerfully. Yusuf got out of the truck and hugged his sister tightly. He kissed the middle of her forehead and pulled away to get a look at her. "Girl, you're looking just as young and as beautiful as you did when we were kids!" Yusuf gushed.

"This crackhead cleans up well, huh!" She laughed.

"Don't say that shit, Yanni." Yusuf frowned. "You need to leave the past in the past, and try to move forward with a brighter look to the future. Speaking of which, yo' boy is here!" Yanni looked at Yusuf, and her smile faded.

"Where he at?" she asked, looking around. "I don't want him to see me yet. I'm not ready, Yusuf!" She looked frightened, and her reaction somewhat surprised him. All Yanni kept talking about was seeing JD for the first time clean and sober, but her reaction seemed to be the exact opposite of her words.

"He's not with me, Yanni," Yusuf assured her. She nervously hugged Yusuf, and it bothered him the way she responded. Maybe it was a good thing that he and JD had gotten into it before he left. The Lord only knows how she would have responded if they'd just shown up unannounced.

CHAPTER SEVEN

"Can you believe that nigga?" Shaggy complained. "How he gone try to manhandle you?"

"I was about to fuck his ass up when you saved him," Willow replied. "I had already kicked him in the nuts, so them muthafuckas was nice and tender for another kneeing!" Shaggy looked at Willow and burst out laughing.

"Why did Cypher wig out on you like that?" Shaggy asked curiously. Willow looked at Shaggy smugly, because at first, she didn't want to tell Shaggy's messy ass. He was telling Duke shit that Willow had told him, and in turn, Duke would call O'Bannon and give him information. Willow didn't have time for any of that shit, because she was hiding out from O'Bannon, and when he used to call with shit, it would really pissed Willow off. She knew she'd fucked him up when she hit him with the car, but she didn't know how badly, which made her very nervous about the entire situation.

"I don't know if I want to tell you, Shaggy. You can't hold water," Willow complained. "I done told you some shit, and it came right back to me."

"Lies and scandal, girl!" Shaggy scoffed, appalled. "I've done nothing of the sort!"

"Girl! Yes, you have!" Willow shot back. "And before you make yourself look stupid. I want you to think back to when we were on tour, and whom you were fucking!" Willow turned her lips up and crossed her arms in front of her chest defensively. Shaggy stared at her for a moment then his eyes widened. "Eeeexactly!" Willow shouted and snapped her fingers in front of Shaggy's face.

"Girl, you ain't got to get all cute and shit! Snapping yo' fingers in my face like that." Shaggy seethed. He turned his lips up at Willow then rolled his eyes. "Okay, Willow, girl. You pointed out my discrepancy, so pardon my vous le vous. Now tell me what you and Cypher were fighting for!" Shaggy demanded. Willow looked at him and laughed.

"I guess I'll forgive you since you're giving me a place to stay." She continued to laugh. "I'm pregnant and—"

"Aaaaaaaaaaaaa!" Shaggy shouted in excitement. "We're going to have a baby! That is totally awesome!" Shaggy jumped up and started dancing around the apartment. He took a feather boa he had hanging on a hook on the wall and wrapped it around his shoulders. Next, he danced and shimmied over to Willow and wrapped her up in it. "We're having a baby! Ooowww! I say a baby!" He pulled the boa back and forth and shimmied in front of Willow happily. Willow stared in amazement because she had never seen Shaggy so relaxed and loose like this. When she saw his outfit, it really clicked for her. It's not every day you see a tall black man in a pair of hot pink workout pants, a white cropped sweatshirt, and some hot pink Ugg boots. She wasn't even aware that they made Uggs that large. "That nigga gone have to pay royally in child support unless you decide to stay here in Cali, which I would prefer if you did!" He noticed the strange look on Willow's face and was taken aback by it. She didn't look excited, and it seemed like she was about to cry. "What's wrong, Willow? Aren't you excited about being pregnant by Cypher?"

Willow looked away for a second then tears rolled down her cheeks.

"That's why we were fighting," Willow sobbed. "Cypher ain't my baby daddy. I'm pregnant by JD, and I miss him so much! It was a mistake for me to come to California, and I need to go back to St. Louis so I can find him." Tears were rushing down her cheeks, and it made Shaggy feel emotional.

"Don't cry, Willow," said Shaggy, wrapping her up in his long arms. He hugged her tightly and sat down on the couch with her. "Shhh, shhh, shhh now, chile! You need to stop all of this crying. That's gone put stress on you and the baby, which you don't need that!"

"I'm sorry, Shaggy," said Willow, wiping her eyes. "But I'm in a jam, and I just don't know what to do. I called myself being honest with Cypher because I wasn't about to fake it with his ass. I'm in love with JD, and we were supposed to be getting married tomorrow."

"Tomorrow! Girl, how you gone get married and you're in California?" asked Shaggy, bluntly. "I guess you could have a FaceTime ceremony, but you won't be able to kiss him when the preacher says, 'You may now kiss the bride.'" Willow sat up and cut her eyes at Shaggy.

"You got fucking jokes I see," Willow scoffed. "I don't know if I want to hit you or hug you right now!" A slight smile played on her lips, and Shaggy smiled warmly at her.

"Miss Willow Autumn Shaw, you need to pull yourself together! That nigga Cypher is mad because you saw him for the phony that he is! Everyone that knows Jesse in real life knows that he ain't no more a gangsta as I am a heterosexual!" Willow pushed Shaggy away and laughed. "I can call my brother Locco over here, and he will tell you that Cypher only talks tough." Willow thought for a second. She didn't feel safe with Cypher being mad at her, and she felt like he could come over at any moment and try to clown her. There was nothing she could really do to defend herself because she knew that she couldn't beat him heads up. He had a weight advantage over her, and that was part of the problem with how he managed to get on top of her and hold her down.

"Let me ask you a question, Shaggy," said Willow, wiping her eyes.

"What's up, buttercup?" Shaggy asked with a caring expression on his face.

"Do you have a gun?" Willow asked with a serious look on her face.

"Why would you ask me something like that?" Shaggy quipped. "Are you going to try to kill my cousin?" He looked at Willow with a very serious expression on his face.

"It all depends," Willow replied. "I won't do it intentionally, but if the nigga came at me aggressively, I would probably shoot his ass in the leg or something."

"Oh," Shaggy replied. He narrowed his eyes at Willow and thought for a second. "He was trying to fuck you up when I came into the room."

"Exactly! So, do you have one?" she asked anxiously.

"Nope," Shaggy admitted. "But I can call my brother and get you one."

"The same brother that everyone is scared of?" asked Willow curiously. "I want to meet him because of the stories y'all told me about him."

"I know for a fact that he'd love your crazy ass!" Shaggy laughed. "His wife is always talking about how Locco is a crazy bitch magnet. She had to shoot a bitch just a few months ago because she was stalking my brother." Willow narrowed her eyes at Shaggy.

"I ain't trying to fuck him. I just want a gun from his ass," Willow scoffed.

"I know, girl." Shaggy huffed. "I'm just making a point to say… never mind. Let me call him."

¤ ¤ ¤ ¤

Knock… Knock… Knock… Shaggy jumped up off the couch and walked over to the door. Willow was in his spare room sleep, and he didn't want to disturb her. He called his brother, Locco, and asked him to come by the house. Shaggy wouldn't tell his brother what he wanted, because it was too risky to talk over the phone. Locco probably would have come over just to smack Shaggy if he'd done some shit like that!

"What the fuck is you doing here?" Shaggy snapped, trying to close the door on Duke.

"Damn, baby! I can't come in to see you?" Duke asked, trying to push through the door.

"I ain't trying to see you right now, Duke," said Shaggy, looking behind him.

"Why are you looking behind you?" Duke spat angrily. "Do you have someone else in here?" Duke gave one big push, and the door flew open. Shaggy fell back against the wall and almost knocked his coat rack over.

"Nigga!" Shaggy yelled in a deep and manly voice. Duke looked at him strangely because Shaggy normally talked in a much lighter, tenor timbre. "You better get the fuck up out of my house before I beat your ass! You done fucked up pushing into my muthafuckin' house like you're crazy or something!"

"Shaggy! What's wrong with your voice?" Duke stammered, sounding surprised.

"That muthafucka was tucked like my dick, bitch!" Shaggy shot back. "Now get the fuck on before I lay these paws on you!" Duke walked toward Shaggy and studied him for a second.

"Say something else in that voice," Duke requested, wrapping his arms around Shaggy's waist. "I think I like that voice better!" Shaggy wasn't trying to hear it at first, but he softened some when Duke moved his hands down to his ass and squeezed it. "You mean to tell me you don't miss me?"

"You know I miss you, Duke." Shaggy caved, rolling his eyes. "I should smack your ass though for knocking me into the coat rack like that."

"Ah, baby," Duke crooned, kissing Shaggy's lips. "Shaggy wrapped his arms around Duke's neck and kissed him back. They were going at it for a few minutes when suddenly, Shaggy pulled back and pushed Duke away from him.

"You have to leave! My big brother is on his way over here, and I don't want him to see you!"

"Locco knows I work for Cypher, so we can play it off," Duke suggested.

"Naw, Duke," said Shaggy nervously, pointing his finger at him. "You's got to go!"

"At least give me one more kiss," Duke insisted. He puckered up his lips, and Willow walked out of the room.

"So… what do we have here?" she smiled. Duke's skin went white when he heard Willow's voice. The cat was out of the bag, or should it be the fag?

CHAPTER EIGHT

*C*harisma was nervous about going to the club with his cousins. Something came up, and they couldn't meet him at the studio. However, they insisted that he come down to the House of Blues on Sunset. Charisma pulled up and noticed Cypher's cousin, Locco, walking into the joint with a few other people. He hoped that Ronnie and Jay weren't planning on joining them, because it would be a very awkward situation.

Shaggy and Willow pulled up to the House of Blues on Sunset to meet up with Locco. Some local rap artist was performing there for the first time, and Locco wanted Shaggy to bring Willow there to meet him. He wasn't sure if Willow was actually a woman, and he didn't want to get jammed up with any of Shaggy's gay shenanigans. Locco didn't care that his little brother was gay. It took a while for him to accept it, but Shaggy was his only little brother, and he couldn't bring himself to turn his back on his blood. Their mother pretended like Shaggy was just like any other red-blooded American man. That's why she forced Shaggy to take a job as Cypher's assistant because she hoped that Cypher could help convince Shaggy to mess with girls. She just refused to accept the fact that he was gayer than Richard Simmons.

"I really ain't in the mood to be at no club," Willow complained.

"I haven't been able to keep anything down, and I hate the fact that I can't even have a fucking drink!"

"Lil' girl, calm your nerves," Shaggy suggested. "We're just going to be here for a little while, and I couldn't exactly tell Locco no. He doesn't understand the word at all!" Willow looked at him and rolled her eyes. "Besides, you need to get out and have some fun! Bitch, you're all the way in Cali-forn-ia! You don't have to worry about O'Dominion or JD, 'cause their asses are in St. Louis!"

"His name is O'Bannon, and JD isn't in St. Louis," Willow explained, correcting him. "O'Bannon is going to find out that I'm in California because your bitch ass man knows that I'm here."

"He ain't gon' say shit, Willow," Shaggy assured her. "That nigga was about to shit on himself when he saw your face!" Shaggy laughed as he checked himself in the rearview mirror."

"I figured you would have dressed a little different," said Willow, smiling. "You look normal as a muthafucka." Shaggy looked at Willow and cut his eyes at her.

"Biiiitch, don't play with me!" Shaggy demanded. "I told you my brother don't play that shit! He probably didn't come to the house, because he thought you were a man, bitch!" Willow frowned up her face and looked at him funny.

"Now, why would he think some shit like that?" asked Willow dryly.

"Because I'm gay, bitch! Keep the fuck up, Willow, damn! You act like you slow or something, and here I am thinking you're one of the sharpest ones in the crayon box," Shaggy scoffed.

"Don't get cute, bitch." Willow chuckled. "'Cause I will embarrass yo' ass with that girly ass jogging suit you got on. I know the difference between the women's suits and the men's, bitch!" Shaggy looked at Willow with his mouth hung open. Willow took her hand and pushed Shaggy's mouth closed. "Close your mouth, Lil' Baby," said Willow. "We don't want any flies to fly into that muthafucka... or random dicks."

"Eeeeeewwww!" Shaggy shouted. "Well, Miss Willow, on that note, I think we need to exit the vehicle before a twirling session begins in this muthafucka!"

"Baby, I don't twirl... I jab," Willow stated frankly then smiled.

"You make me sick, you know that?" Shaggy hissed, rolling his eyes at her. "And, if you didn't know it, I just wanted to let you know!" Willow laughed and pushed Shaggy on the arm.

"Thank you," said Willow, and she laid her head on his arm.

"Get off of me," scoffed Shaggy jerking his arm away.

"I don't like your ass." Willow laughed as she opened the car door.

"Whatever, Shaggy," said Willow, getting out of the car. "You just better hope I don't decide to clown you in this club."

"Girl, you better not! 'Cause I will surely leave your little pregnant, skanky ass here at this club to get a ride from a random stranger." Shaggy chuckled.

"Yo' brother would take me home," said Willow confidently then she laughed.

"Girl that nigga would take you to his apartment," Shaggy scoffed. "But you better hope none of his hoes show up at that muthafucka looking for his ass!"

"Yo' brother must be fine," said Willow, straightening her skirt.

"Yes, he is," Shaggy replied arrogantly. "It runs in the family."

Shaggy and Willow walked into the packed club and made their way to the bar. They ordered something to drink then Shaggy cased the place to see if he could find Locco. He noticed Charisma sitting over at a table with his cousins, and Shaggy wanted to avoid them at all cost. Every time Shaggy ran into Jay, he would be a complete asshole toward Shaggy and always tried to ridicule him.

"Let's go this way," said Shaggy. "He's probably sitting close to the stage."

"There's a lot of people here," said Willow, looking around the place. "And the crowd is turnt up!"

"Ain't they though?" Shaggy agreed. He felt someone touch his shoulder, and it scared the living daylights out of him. Shaggy swung around on his heels ready to act a fool, but it was his big brother standing behind him with a smile on his face. "Boy! You was about to get these paws." Shaggy huffed.

"You wasn't gon' do shit, Shaggy." Locco laughed.

"He probably wasn't, but I was gone get yo' ass together," Willow countered. Locco turned and looked at Willow smugly. He liked the feisty ass chocolate chick that was mean mugging him up and down.

"Who's this little chocolate chip?" asked Locco, clocking Willow.

He liked the way her cotton miniskirt hugged her hips, and the half tank top that she wore had plenty of spillage as her breasts hung over the top of it generously. "What's yo' name, baby?"

"I don't give that type information to random strangers," she replied. "What's yo' name?" Locco looked back at Shaggy and laughed.

"I love her," Locco proclaimed, laughing. "Aye! You with me tonight." He wrapped his arm around Willow's waist and looked down at her. He was six feet eight and weighed about 350 pounds solid. His muscles were ripped, and they were marked up like the graffiti-filled walls on Venice Beach.

"Locco, this my friend, Willow, that I told you about," Shaggy announced and laughed.

"Nice to meet you, Willow," said Locco, smiling at her.

"It's nice to meet your acquaintance, Locco, but my man wouldn't take too kindly with you hugging all on me like this and shit," Willow replied.

"Where yo' man at?" Locco asked, looking around. "Is that nigga here?"

"Naw, that nigga's somewhere in the middle of the map," she replied smugly.

"So, if yo' man ain't here, then don't trip," said Locco arrogantly. "My wife is at home with our kids, but you don't see me trippin'."

"That's the difference between me and you," Willow scoffed. "My nigga ain't got to be with me in order for me to be loyal." Locco tightened his grip on Willow's waist and smiled.

"I'm telling you, Shaggy. I'm in love," Locco crooned and laughed. "Come on, lil' mama. You gone be my date tonight, and I don't give a fuck if you do have a man. Tell that nigga to come see me if he has a problem with it!" Willow looked at him and smiled.

"You don't want those problems," Willow assured him. "Yo' ass is swole, and my baby is way smaller than you, but he'd gun yo' ass down like a big game hunter!" Locco, Shaggy, and Willow laughed hysterically. "But as long as you're respectful, then we don't have shit to worry about."

"I'm always a gentleman, lil' mama," Locco assured her then smiled. He put his hand down and took Willow's inside of his. "I got a table over by the stage. Let's go have a seat."

****

Charisma was walking around the club and noticed Willow and Shaggy sitting over at a table with Locco and his best friend, Warren. Willow was sitting kind of close to Locco, and he wondered if she was fucking with him now. It was strange that Cypher wasn't there with them, and he wondered if Cypher even knew that Willow was in Cali. He pulled out his phone and dialed Cypher's number. He noticed Locco leaning over, and he whispered something in Willow's ear. She placed her hand on his thigh and laughed enthusiastically. It looked like they were a couple, and Charisma couldn't believe his eyes.

"Hello."

"Where are you?" asked Charisma, watching the pair.

"I'm at home. Why?" asked Cypher curiously.

"Did you know that Willow's in Cali 'cause I'm staring right at her?" Charisma questioned.

"Yeah, I know she's here," Cypher scoffed. "I picked that bitch up from the airport two days ago."

"Well, I'm at the House of Blues on Sunset, and she's sitting all cozy-like with your cousin, Locco," Charisma informed him.

"For real!" Cypher yelled angrily. "I can't believe that little fag, Shaggy! He came and got Willow earlier from my house. I should have known that bitch ass nigga was goin' to try to pull some shit like that!"

"Why did she leave your house with Shaggy and not you?" Charisma questioned being nosy.

"Because... we had a disagreement."

"About what?" asked Charisma, steady prying. "I'm just surprised that she's here without that nigga... What's his name?"

"Man, fuck that nigga! That's his name," Cypher snapped. "Besides, I really don't give a fuck what she does! I hope that bitch chokes on that nigga Locco's little dick!"

"That just might happen, my friend," Charisma reassured him. "That just might happen!"

CHAPTER NINE

"*I* don't know why this girl ain't picking up her phone," JD fussed. "I know she ain't fake a fallout so that she could be laid up with that nigga, letting him touch all over her ass!"

"JD, calm down," Yusuf advised. "You said it yourself that Willow was loyal to you. Why would you think that she would be laid up with some dude?"

"'Cause they got a little history together, and she's pissed off at me," JD replied with a grimace on his face. "It's complicated."

"Whenever something has to do with a woman, it's always complicated," Yusuf agreed and laughed. "I just want you to calm down and go about things a different way. You should have faith in your queen, especially since you seem to have so much faith in her when you're going out to handle business." JD looked at his uncle skeptically.

"I hear what you're saying, but you know how niggas are." JD frowned. "If it was me, and I knew that the pussy was golden..." JD looked at his uncle smugly. "Shiiidddd, I'm goin' to try to slide up in that shit!" Yusuf gave JD some dap and laughed.

"Young blood, you talk like yo' gal's pussy is worth its weight in gold," Yusuf replied still laughing. JD looked at him with the most serious expression on his face.

"We talking tight and damn near virginal," JD proclaimed. "But that's not even the point, Unc. Willow is my everything, and she makes a nigga wanna change his life. She's carrying my shorty, and…" JD looked off into the woods and sighed. "We were supposed to be getting married tomorrow."

"Well, we know that shit ain't gone happen," Yusuf uttered. JD glared at his uncle and frowned.

"If I go to California and get her ass, it will!" JD declared.

"I can't wait to meet this young lady," said Yusuf, pulling out a cigarette. He fired it up and took a pull of it.

"Nigga, you know Willow," JD scoffed. "She lived across the hall from us with her mother and brother."

"Wait a minute! Didn't her brother get killed trying to protect they mama? Uhhhh, what was they mama's name? Melody! They mama's name was Melody, and she got a life sentence for killing the nigga that killed her son!"

"Exactly!" JD agreed.

"But I thought shorty belonged to O'Bannon," Yusuf recalled. "Didn't Melody work out some deal for him to take care of Willow or something like that?"

"Well, the deal is off!" JD replied full of conviction. "Willow broke free from that nigga, and he's having a hard time accepting the shit. The nigga tried to kill me, and Lil' Baby handled his ass with my car! That's why we laying low for a while."

"Did she kill him?"

"Nope!" JD replied. "KC said she just fucked him up a little. His left leg is shattered, and I think he said his shoulder is fucked up, but I don't even care for real. The nigga tried to sneak up and dome me!"

"That nigga did what!" shouted Yusuf, outraged. "You should have went and made sure the nigga was dead before you drove off; put a couple of slugs in his head! What did I teach you about leaving loose ends?"

"I know, Unc, but I was a bit shook up cause my life flashed before my eyes. I swear to God, I would have had my head on flat if that nigga would have let loose a second earlier. That's why I love my Lil' Baby 'til the death of me! She is my world, and I can't stand being away from her! I had no problems sleeping alone before Willow happened," JD admitted. "I'd have a lil' thot stop by, knock her down, and send her ass home when we were done, but now, Unc… "JD looked at him sadly. "I can't even sleep right. I'm used to feeling her warm body next to mine." JD stopped talking, and his thoughts drifted off to the love of his life. "Man, I miss her! Willow has the softest skin, and it always smells like cocoa butter. I loved rolling over and sliding my dick inside of her in the middle of the night. She'd just lift her leg a little and push her ass back so a nigga can slide on in!"

"Uh, nephew… I don't need to know all of that," Yusuf uttered uncomfortably.

"My bad, Unc! I just miss my bitch, and I want her here with me!" JD sighed. "She needs to answer her muthafuckin' phone before I hit the highway and sniff her ass out like a Saint Bernard looking for cocaine!"

"That sounds serious," Yusuf scoffed.

"As a muthafuckin' heart attack!" JD agreed.

"I hope you find her, nephew," Yusuf offered. "I was going to talk to you about something, but I'm gon' wait until after you find yo' boo." JD looked at him curiously.

"You ain't got to wait," JD replied.

"Yes, I do. I'll just come check back with you later," Yusuf promised. He got up out of his chair and patted JD on his back. "You've always been a passionate dude." JD frowned at his uncle.

"Huh?" JD scoffed.

"I'm talking about in reference to believing deeply in something," Yusuf explained.

"Ah." JD smiled. Yusuf walked in the house to leave JD to his thoughts. He knew that now wasn't a good time to talk to JD about his mother. Maybe once he'd found Willow, he'd be more open to discussing Yanni.

JD sat for a second, thinking about the last time he held Willow in his arms. He felt like he was being a soft ass nigga but even gangstas needed love too. He reached into his pocket and pulled out his phone. He wondered if Keena had talked to Willow because if at least one of them have talked to her, he would feel much better about the situation.

"What's the word, big homie?" Keena spat.

"What's the word, Keena?" JD replied. "Have you talked to my wife?"

"Nigga, it ain't official yet." Keena laughed.

"Don't play," JD replied. "You know that's my bitch forever!"

"Yo' bitch, huh?" Keena laughed. "You better not let her hear you say that!"

"And yo' ass betta not tell her I said it either!" JD scoffed. "She's pissed off and hung the phone up on me, but for real, Keena, have you talked to Willow?" She heard a bit of desperation in his voice, so she figured she'd better probe him.

"What's wrong, JD? Why did she hang up on you?"

"She's pissed at me because I left her in St. Louis. I called her phone several times after, and she still ain't answer. I checked all her social media pages, and she ain't been on none of that shit in days."

"Do you think that nigga, Cypher, got her locked up in a room or something?" asked Keena, sounding worried herself.

"Why would you say something like that?" asked JD, concerned. "I don't think that soft ass nigga would do anything like that to her. He loves Willow's dirty drawls, so he probably got her ass livin' lavish or some shit." JD got quiet for a second. "Do you think Willow would choose to be with that nigga?"

"I hope not!" Keena quipped. "Remember that nigga raped me, and he's no good, JD! Willow would never pick that nigga over you! She loves you too much!"

"Don't remind me about that shit, 'cause I get pissed off every time I think about the shit!" JD fussed. "You just better make sure the next time some shit like that happens, you let us make the muthafuckin' decision on whether or not we want to ride for you! Call that flunky ass nigga, Charisma, and find out if he knows where my queen is, and call me back!" JD hung up the phone and punched his fist through the glass storm door. Yusuf walked up and looked down at the mess. He could see his nephew was going insane about his woman, and he figured he might be able to do something about it.

CHAPTER TEN

"*W*here the fuck you been?" O'Bannon snapped. "The detectives just left, and I told them you had some information for them." Patsy looked at O'Bannon uncomfortably.

"My fault, O. I had to take care of some business. How the fuck you think we gone pay these hospital bills? The first surgery they gave you cost over $200,000, and the hospital stay with you being hooked up to all of these machines is at least $60,000."

"Bitch, do you think I'm concerned about any of that shit?" O'Bannon retorted through clenched teeth. "Hoe, I make that shit every day, so don't be coming at me with trivial, petty bullshit like that! You just better make sure muthafuckas making their drops and my shit getting picked up!"

"I am, O, damn! You ain't got to cuss me like that!" Patsy complained, frowning. "This shit is stressful as fuck! You got me scared as hell that a muthafucka might try to do something to me!"

"Ain't nobody stuntin' yo' black ass! Yo' cousin's bitch did this shit to me trying to save her man's life. I can't believe Willow would do some shit like this to me over JD's black, raggedy ass! I wanted to give that bitch the world, but for some reason, she's in love with a twenty-five-cent ass nigga!"

"Don't talk about my cousin," Patsy scoffed. "JD's got it goin' on, but see, you wouldn't know because you one of those stupid ass, flashy niggas. You got to ride around in luxury cars and live in the biggest damn house in the county, drawing attention to your already convicted felon looking ass!" O'Bannon looked at Patsy in disbelief. He couldn't believe that she was talking to him like that.

"Who the fuck you talking to, Patsy?" O'Bannon questioned angrily. "Don't think 'cause I'm hooked up to all of this shit that I won't fuck you up!" He glared at Patsy angrily because if he wasn't in that bed, she wouldn't be so blatantly disrespectful. "Aye, Ricky, come here!" Ricky stepped in the room and stood at the foot of the bed. "Grab that bitch and bring her to me." Ricky lifted an eyebrow at him. "You heard what the fuck I said! Bring that black bitch to me!" Ricky looked over at Patsy with an indifferent look on his face. He grabbed Patsy by her shoulders and pushed her across the floor. She tried to plant her feet firmly, and they slid across the linoleum tiles as Ricky moved her body like he was pushing something on a dolly.

"O'Bannon, no!" Patsy protested, putting up her hands. His cell phone rang, and he looked over at it annoyingly. He turned back around and slapped the shit out Patsy. The hit made her eardrum ring, and the skin on the side of her face burned from the hard impact of O'Bannon's hand. Tears instantly fell from her eyes, and the taste of blood in her mouth made her put her hand up to her lips.

"Get the fuck out my face!" O'Bannon howled. He picked up the phone and answered, "Hello."

"I got some news that I think you want to hear," Duke gloated. "Willow is here in California! I saw her earlier, and she didn't look too enthused about being here!"

"When did she get there?" O'Bannon asked.

"I don't know, but I saw her at Shaggy's house. I went there to handle some business, and she came out of the back. It looked like she was sleep or something, and Cypher wasn't with her. Shaggy said Willow was going to spend a couple of days with her... I mean him."

"I want you to bring that bitch to me!" O'Bannon demanded. "I don't give a fuck how you get her here. Just bring the bitch to me!"

"You know it's really going to cost you, O'Bannon. I'm about to commit several felonies and risk my freedom for you. Willow ain't an easy bitch to snatch and bring back to St. Louis, you know?" Duke explained. "And her boyfriend is a muthafucka too! Shiiiddd, but yo' ass already know! You in the fucking hospital because of the two of them!" O'Bannon had Ricky reach out to Duke when the shit first happened and told him to keep an eye out for Willow. O'Bannon knew that there was a chance that Willow would run to Cypher. He was far enough away from St. Louis but not far enough! "Let me check some shit out and then I'll give you a price. Your ass gone have to pay for expenses and everything, and I want my money up front. No bullshitting! You won't fuck me over on this one!"

"Agreed. Call me back," O'Bannon seethed then hung up. He was pissed off about the entire situation all the way around. He was going to have to pay Duke's sleazy ass to bring Willow back to him, not to mention the fact that Duke might be a liability. O'Bannon was going to pay the nigga whatever he wanted to do the job, but when he delivered Willow to him, he was going to have Ricky kill that nigga to clean up any loose ends.

****

Patsy got in her car and pulled the visor down. She looked at her face and saw the damage that O'Bannon did to it. She pressed her tongue against her cheek to puff it out to get a better look at the bruising. The cut on her bottom lip wasn't that big, but it burned like a muthafucka. She was furious and couldn't believe that Ricky would do some shit like that. She thought that their relationship was stronger due to the fact that they were fucking now. Maybe she needed to step her game up because if she planned on taking over the promotion business without any resistance from O'Bannon, she needed to solidify an ally amongst O's flock. Pasty was dark skinned, so the bruising wasn't that noticeable. Her concealer would hide it, so she wasn't worried about anyone seeing it. It was hurtful to hear that O'Bannon wanted to give Willow everything, and she was actually his wife. She knew that he loved Willow, but damn! O'Bannon just didn't give a fuck anymore, and throwing shit up in her face was nothing to him! She was so deep in thought that she didn't see Ricky walking up to the car. He grabbed the door handle and lifted it, but it didn't open.

"Aye, open the door!" Ricky demanded. Patsy nervously hit the button and unlocked it. Ricky opened up the door and climbed inside. He grabbed her face by the chin and surveyed the damage. "I'm sorry, Black Cherry," Ricky apologized. "But I had to do what O'Bannon said; he's my boss."

"I know, baby," Patsy assured him. She wasn't really in an understanding mood, but she knew what game to play. "It's not as bad as it looks. A little makeup will do the trick."

"Come here," said Ricky, pulling her into his arms. He hugged her tightly and kissed her forehead. "You need to take that hair out it stinks." Pasty pulled away from him and frowned.

"I went to work out this morning and didn't have time to wash my hair," Pasty whispered. "I thought you were down for me, but all you wanted was some pussy!"

"I thought that's what you wanted to give me, Patsy. You're the one walking around in your underwear and skimpy clothes in front of me!"

"That's my fucking house, so I can wear whatever the fuck I want!" Patsy fussed. "Ain't nobody tell you to be watching me like that anyway!"

"But that's what I'm paid for," Ricky spat back. "To watch your pretty black ass, so stop fussing and give me some sugar!" Patsy cut her eyes at him and stuck her bottom lip out.

"Owww!" Patsy winced. "I can't even kiss you. My fuckin' mouth hurts!"

"Let me see," said Ricky, staring at her face. He studied it for a moment then kissed her on the cheek. He kissed the other side then pulled away and looked at her hungrily. He lusted for Patsy because he thought she was the most beautiful black creature that he'd ever seen. Ricky's family was straight from Africa, and Patsy's ebony skin reminded him of his beloved grandmother over in Kenya.

"I need to know that I can trust you, Ricky, to protect me! I don't want to interfere with your job, but I will pay you extra if I have to," Patsy pleaded.

"Did you ever think that maybe I don't want money," Ricky shot back. He slid his hand inside of Patsy's deep V T-shirt and fondled her breasts. He licked his lips hungrily as Patsy watched him. She understood perfectly what Ricky was implying, and she was going to use it to her advantage. She pressed the button and let her seat recline. Next, she spread her legs open wide, welcoming a peek of her goodies to Ricky. She bit her bottom lip suggestively and smiled wickedly when he stared anxiously. He was geeked up that Patsy was being so accommodating to his desires, and he planned on taking full advantage of the situation by enjoying Patsy's offerings.

Ricky took his free hand and gripped Patsy's thigh. He licked his lips lasciviously as he slid his hand up her leg and brushed his finger against the fabric of her panties. He slid his finger under the elastic and plunged it inside of her wet walls. Patsy groaned deeply as Ricky put another one up in her. He slid them in and out of her aching pussy, and Patsy groaned in desire because it felt so good.

"This pussy could be all yours, Ricky," Patsy sang. "O ain't lovin' me right, and you know it." Ricky pulled his fingers out and put them in his mouth. He dragged them down his tongue and marveled at the exquisite taste of Patsy's nectar. Next, he drove his fingers back deep inside of her and kissed her lips passionately.

"You ain't gone have to worry about shit, Patsy. I'm gone take care of you," Ricky uttered breathlessly.

"You promise?" she moaned.

"I put that on my life," Ricky replied. "It's gone be me and you against the world!"

CHAPTER ELEVEN

"Hello."

"Hey, Charisma, I hate to disturb you, but you wouldn't happen to be around Willow, would you?" Keena asked abruptly.

"It's funny that you should ask me that. I'm actually at a club, and I saw her here with Shaggy and his brother."

"Is Cypher with them?" Keena asked wearily.

"Nope. He's nowhere in sight, which is strange to me," Charisma mentioned. "I'm surprised that Cypher wasn't being quite protective of Willow around Locco." He'd already talked to Cypher and knew what was going on but decided to play dumb to see if he could get more information.

"Why do you say that?" asked Keena curiously.

"Because, she and Locco look real cozy up in this muthafucka," Charisma chuckled. "I guess she's passing that pussy around to any nigga that she thinks is a gangsta."

"Nigga, what?" Keena snapped, pissed. "You got my bestie fucked up! She ain't loose like me, and she damn sure ain't gone be passing her pussy out like that, ole lame ass nigga!"

"Damn! I'm sorry, Keena," Charisma apologized. "I was just saying."

"Don't just say shit about my patna'!" Keena spat. "Now, take yo' weak ass over to her table and give her the phone! You betta hope I don't tell her what ya' ass said about her!"

"Who the fuck you talkin' to like that, ole rat bitch!" Charisma retorted. "You got me completely fucked up!" Charisma hung up on Keena and stared at his phone in complete disbelief. A frown came across his face because he was curious to know why Willow wasn't answering her phone. He took a swig of his beer and looked back at his cousins. Ronnie was playing games, and he didn't have time to be hanging out with their ignorant asses. Charisma knew they only wanted him to come out with them to foot the bill, but he had a surprise for them mooching muthafuckas.

Charisma finished his beer and sat it on the bar. He walked toward the table where Willow was sitting and was abruptly stopped by two dudes that were clearly Locco's guys. The men stared him down and bucked up like they were about to beat Charisma's ass.

"He's cool, y'all," Shaggy spoke up. "He works for Cypher." The men gave him another once over and moved out of the way to let him pass.

"Thanks, Shaggy," Charisma uttered, looking leery. "What's up?"

"Shit," Shaggy replied. "What brings you here?"

"I came to hang out with my cousins, Ronnie and Jay," Charisma explained.

"Jay's with you?" asked Shaggy smugly. "Where he at?"

"Over there on the other side of the stage. I'm trying to hide from his ass 'cause they're treating me like an ATM machine," Charisma complained. Shaggy looked at him unsympathetically and laughed. "Who are you here with besides your brother's bodyguards?"

"Locco is here, and those ain't his bodyguards. They're just his homeboys that came with him," Shaggy explained. "He went with Willow out to the car."

"Damn! She don't waste no time moving to the next hot nigga, huh?" Charisma chuckled. Shaggy looked at him, annoyed.

"What da fuck you mean?" asked Shaggy defensively. "Willow left her phone in the car, and Locco didn't want her walking out there by herself. She and Cypher had gotten into it real bad, and my brother wanted to make sure that Willow was safe, especially since she's pregnant. Catch that dirty!" Shaggy snapped his finger in front of Charisma's face and frowned with his lips poked out. "Why would you think that Willow was a hoe? She never presented herself as such, and the one that you should be calling a hoe is that one you was fucking!"

"I didn't mean to offend you, Shaggy, fuck! I was just saying that because Willow was fucking with Cypher and JD at the same damn time!"

"Correction! Willow wasn't fucking both of them at the same time. JD told Willow to go see if she liked Cypher, and if shit didn't work out, then come on home! Apparently, Cypher's bullshit came to a head, and Willow found out that the nigga was really a phony for real."

"Aye, you know I'm hip! I told that nigga that the shit was going to catch up with him. He's walking around trying to act like his ass is

Locco or somebody," Charisma complained. "You know I helped that nigga write his rhymes, and he tried to play me like a poo butt!"

"I heard y'all arguing. I was the one who made the recording that Indigo had," Shaggy confessed. "I was on the tour bus when you guys were going at it, and I felt like it was some good shit to have."

"That's how that video got made. The nigga tried to say that I did the shit, but I pointed out the angle would be impossible for me to do it, but that nigga's been acting real strange and shit. I don't know what's going on with him, but he better get it together!"

"The nigga is an alcoholic; that's his problem," Shaggy replied. "But his ass will be okay." Charisma looked to see if he could see Willow walking around. It was taking them a long time to come back inside, and he wondered if everyone had Willow pegged wrong.

Locco asked Willow to go take a ride with him, so they could grab what she wanted from him. She was a little nervous at first but figured she was with the safest muthafucka around the way by how everyone talked about him. This was the nigga that Cypher pretended to be, so she was curious to know the man behind the myth.

"They talk about you like you're God or something," Willow spat and smiled.

"I am," Locco replied. "Niggas know that I ain't to be fucked with."

"I see how people respond to you, but I ain't impressed," Willow joked. He looked at her arrogantly.

"Is that right?" Locco chuckled. "I heard some shit about you, but I ain't impressed."

"I ain't trying to impress you," Willow replied rudely. "I just want to get a heater from you so I can truly feel safe around this muthafucka."

"Why don't you feel safe. baby girl?" Locco asked curiously.

"'Cause Cypher's got me fucked up!" she replied. "That nigga put his hands on me, and I don't play that shit! My king would dead that nigga if he knew Cypher put his hands on me."

"I heard a little something about him too," Locco replied. "Shaggy said y'all make quite the pair."

"We be Crippin in our neighborhood," Willow gloated and laughed.

"Ah, yeah, ma?" Locco laughed. "What set you claim?"

"I claim 42 Kitchen Crip," Willow spat, throwing up her set. Locco got a kick out of watching Willow because all the niggas he knew from St. Louis was always quick to throw up their set.

"You St. Louis niggas know y'all be representing!"

"Ain't no other way," Willow replied. "Cali niggas be the craziest... sike!" They both laughed as they jumped on the freeway. "Where we goin'?"

"To handle some business. It'll only take a few minutes," Locco replied. "You cool with that? I'll throw you a few dollars." Willow looked at him strangely.

"Why did you think I would be cool with this?" Willow questioned.

"'Cause St. Louis bitches are the craziest!" Locco sang. Willow laughed at him and sat back in her seat.

"Since you got me riding with you to handle business, then you gotta tell me about yo' self," Willow insisted. "So, get to talking!" Locco looked at Willow and smiled.

"Alright, ma," he replied. "What you wanna know?"

Locco started telling Willow about his humble beginnings and how he got into the gang life. He talked about how his loyalty and dedication to the game brought him prosperity, pleasure, and pain. He had to serve ten years in a federal penitentiary when he was seventeen years old, and that's where he learned all the rules to the game and life while serving time. He mentioned being locked up with a crazy nigga named Twin from St. Louis. Locco mentioned that Twin was from over her way, and she may know some of his family members. He told Willow that Twin had a nephew that was doin' it on the Northside, but Willow told him if he didn't have a name, then she wouldn't know. Locco laughed at her response because she was too hip for her own good. Locco was forty-two but looked like he was thirty-two. He had a low cut that was connected to a long beard that reached his chest. He looked like a big old teddy bear to Willow, and he even reminded her of her deceased brother. They were well acquainted with one another after their not so short ride, and they even made plans for Locco to come visit her in St. Louis with a care package of all things green and wonderful!

CHAPTER TWELVE

*L*occo pulled up in front of a house that looked like Smokey's from the movie *Friday*. It tripped Willow out because all of the houses had the same screen door on them. The only thing that was different was the colors because some of the houses had black, and the others had white. Willow wanted to get out of the car, run up to the door, and knock on it because she was gone beat on it just like Smokey did.

"We're here," Locco announced. He put the truck in park and reached under the seat. He pulled out his pistol then checked the clip. Willow stared at him questionably, because she wasn't sure what the fuck was going on.

"You pulling out weapons and shit. Where mines at?" Willow questioned. Locco looked over at her and lifted an eyebrow. "Don't look at me like that! If yo' big swole ass got a hammer, then I want one too! I ain't going in there blindly!"

"I ain't got nothing small, Willow," he replied, pulling out another pistol. "And that outfit you got on ain't made to carry no gun."

"You got me fucked up on my dead brother!" Willow spat. "I ain't going in there without shit!" Willow looked at the door then back at Locco.

"I promise ain't shit gone happen to you, Willow," Locco promised. "We just coming to pick up some money, and I'll throw in a little something extra." Willow looked in the side mirror and cased her surroundings. She liked to know what the fuck was going down from the jump so she could prepare herself mentally. "What's up? You coming?" Willow stared at Locco for a second then snatched the gun out of his hand. She sat it on the floor, out of sight then grabbed the door handle.

"Just in case we have to run up out that muthafucka," Willow scoffed. Locco laughed as he got out of the truck.

"I like your way of thinking," Locco laughed. He walked around and opened Willow's door. She took a deep breath and climbed out of the truck. "It's going to be fine, ma. Let's go."

Locco and Willow walked up to the house. He looked and nodded for her to knock on the door. A big smile spread across her face because this was something that she really wanted to do. Willow took her fist and beat on the door rapidly like she was the DEA or somebody. Locco laughed because he could tell that Willow was really enjoying it.

"Who the fuck—Oh, Locco, it's you."

"What's up?" Locco laughed. "You got to excuse my friend. She's from out of town and autistic." Willow spun around on her heels and stared at Locco with a scowl on her face. Locco furrowed his brow and nodded his head as if to say go along with it. "Come on, Lisa. Follow me," Locco directed, walking into the house. Willow remembered that she had a knife in her little purse and wanted to go back to get it.

"Can you hit the locks? I forgot my candy," Willow replied. Locco looked at her strangely. "Please!"

"Okay, hurry up," Locco instructed, hitting the chirp. He walked inside of the house while the dude who opened the door stepped out for a second and looked around. Willow watched him carefully before she got in the truck, then he shut the screen door behind him and left the other one cracked. She hurried and climbed inside because she didn't want anyone seeing what she was getting. Her knife would fit discreetly in her bra, and they wouldn't even know she had it. Willow slid it down in her cleavage and adjusted herself meticulously. She was about to get out of the truck when she saw something suspicious. A car pulled up in front of the truck, and a guy jumped out of it. He ran around toward the back of the house, and the driver remained inside of the vehicle, looking very suspicious and nervous. Willow wasn't stupid, and she felt like maybe Locco had a little gangsta party planned for her, but she remembered the one thing that Locco told her about him is that he don't play games with no muthafucka. He's a man of his word, but a lot of niggas don't like him for that, so he always had to watch his back.

Willow grabbed the gun off the floor and scooted down off the seat. She opened the door slightly and climbed out, trying to be discreet. She left it cracked and walked down the side of the truck and crept around the back to get a better look at the driver. She placed the gun under her arm with only the handle sticking out and kept her hand on the handle and trigger just in case she had to put in some work.

"Excuse me," Willow giggled. "Do you have a cigarette?" She

walked up to the window and smiled at the man giddily.

"Bitch, I don't smoke! Get the fuck away from here!" he spat, sounding agitated.

"Wrong answer," said Willow as she pulled out the gun and placed it against his head. She stepped to the side and pulled the trigger letting off two shots in his head. She quickly ducked down and ran back over to the truck. She went around to the back of it and watched the house for a second. No one came to the door, and that made her nervous. It surprised her that no one came to see what was going on, so she knew Locco might be in trouble.

Willow thought for a second and figured going in through the back might be the best course of action. She tripped off the way Locco reached in the back of the truck and grabbed a second gun, so she wondered was there anything else back there that she could use. Willow dipped back on the driver's side and went to the back door. She opened it up and was wowed when she saw a duffle bag full of guns.

"Hot damn!" shouted Willow as she grabbed two more pistols and shoved them in her waistband. She reached deeper inside and found a baby Uzi that reminded her of the one JD kept in Helter Skelter. "Now we're talking!"

Willow took one of the guns out of her waist and put it back. She grabbed another clip and placed it in the back of her skirt in case she had to spray the entire room. She shut the truck door behind her and ran to the side of the house. She peeked inside a window and noticed Locco sitting on the couch. The man who opened the door had a shotgun pointed at Locco, and the other man who ran in the house had a pistol on him too. They were yelling and cursing at Locco, but he was just sitting there calmly as if nothing was going on. Willow knew that she ran the risk of getting Locco shot, but if she didn't do anything, she wouldn't feel right. He was Shaggy's brother, and Shaggy came to her rescue more than once. Willow knew she was built for this shit, and if it were JD, he would do the same thing.

"You need to tell us what time they coming to the other house, so we can be there waiting," said the man holding the shotgun.

"Anthony, I can't believe you gone cross me like this," Locco fussed, "after all that I've done for you."

"Nigga, this business," Anthony replied. "You sitting fat, and the rest of us just living day to day."

"You know you sound like a bitch ass nigga." Locco chuckled.

"Fuck you, Locco!" Anthony spat. "Where the fuck did that bitch go? It's taking her a long time to come in the house."

"I told you, I didn't see nobody out there," said the dude who came through the door.

"Go see if you see her, Rabbit," Anthony instructed. "You should have gone to see who was out there shooting. It might have been that bitch!" Rabbit put his gun down into his pants and walked toward the door. Willow was standing in the back of the house in the shadows and planned to make her move when the one guy walked out of the house. Anthony had lowered his shotgun down toward the floor because he didn't have plans on shooting Locco. Rabbit opened the door followed by the screen door and walked out, closing it behind him. Anthony looked toward the window and watched Rabbit walk to the car. Willow pressed her back against the wall and slid down it with the pistol in her hand. She was a relatively good shot because JD made sure they got target practice in at the range. Willow knew that it was of grave importance to at least fuck ole boy up, or else both she and Locco might get fucked up. She took a deep breath and grabbed for the door handle. Luckily, it was locked, and she slid up into the house inconspicuously.

Pow... Pow... Pow... Pow... Pow... Gunshots sounded off in the house, and Locco dropped down to his knees, pulling out his gun. Willow rushed in after letting off her shots, and Locco turned toward Anthony to load his ass up, but Anthony was lying on the floor with half of his head blown off. Rabbit ran inside of the house, and Willow unloaded three shots in his chest, and Locco hit him with five. She saw a bag of money sitting on the table next to where she was standing and decided that it needed to go with her.

"Come on, nigga! Let's get the fuck out of here!" Willow shouted.

Willow threw the Uzi in the bag of money, swooped it up, and ran toward the back of the house. Locco hit his locks and followed her but kept looking back to see if anyone was coming behind them. They dashed out the back door and headed toward the alley.

"Follow me," said Locco, grabbing her hand. They ran down the alley to the left and ducked into the backyard about six houses down.

"Why you got us in this yard?" Willow whispered, sounding a bit agitated. "We're sitting ducks!"

"Chill, ma," Locco cooed. "This my people's house."

Willow looked at him strangely and rolled her eyes. She pulled the other gun and clip out of her waist and put it in the bag. She zipped it up and looked up at Locco with a serious expression on her face.

"What's yo' plan? We're just goin' to sit here and wait?" Willow hissed.

"Yeah," Locco whispered, sounding frustrated.

"Wrong answer," Willow scoffed. She walked passed Locco and cased the yard. She saw a big screwdriver and grabbed it off the ground. "I'll be right back," said Willow, attempting to walk past him. Locco grabbed her arm and pulled her toward him.

"Where you going?" Locco asked, annoyed. "We cool waiting right here. Trust me!" Willow's eyes widened.

"Trusting you got us right here, nigga!" Willow snapped. She jerked away and walked out in the alley. She hid the screwdriver under her arm and disappeared out of sight. Locco shook his head because he knew that they were safe, but for some reason, Willow didn't want to believe it. Locco pulled out his phone and texted his cousin, telling him that he was in his backyard. Locco told him not to come out but to unlock the back door because he'd be sliding inside with a friend. Locco was pissed off about the entire situation because he didn't expect an ambush. Luckily for him, Willow was a savage, and she handled the situation like a real G! Locco looked out in the alley and heard people talking loudly. He knew the police would be arriving soon, and the damn girl just ran off. Locco sat down on a little stoop and pulled out a blunt. He was going to wait for Willow to come back, then they would go into the house together.

CHAPTER THIRTEEN

*J*D decided to take a walk around his land to clear his head. Keena called back and told him that Willow was staying with Shaggy, but something had happened, and Charisma couldn't talk. This infuriated him because it felt like he was constantly being slapped in the face for making the wrong decision. He had a bad feeling in the pit of his stomach and felt like Willow was in trouble. He hit his blunt and let the smoke linger in his lungs for a second before he blew it out. All he wanted to do was talk to Willow and then cuss her ass out for not answering any of his calls.

"JD!" shouted Yusuf, coming toward him. He was riding on an ATV and pulled up on JD. "Damn! Didn't you hear me calling you?"

"Apparently not if I ain't answer," JD scoffed.

"We need to go back to the house, so you can take this call," Yusuf explained. "And, nigga, you owe me for making this possible."

"Who the fuck am I about to talk to, former President Obama or something?" JD asked sarcastically.

"Your ass is silly, you know that? You'll see. Now, come the fuck on," Yusuf demanded. JD climbed on the back of it apprehensively, and they rode back to the house.

****

Willow pulled up to the house where Locco was hiding in the backyard. She let down the window and searched the area for Locco. The one thing that Cali niggas and St. Louis niggas shared in common was a love for old school cars. She binked a 1989 Cutlass Ciera with the screwdriver, and it felt like she was taking candy from a baby.

"Aye, Locco! Hoodie hoo!" Willow called out. Locco stepped out the yard and looked at the car.

"Where the fuck you get this from?" Locco asked, smiling.

"Don't worry about it," she replied. "Grab that bag, and let's get the fuck out of here! The police just arrived, and it looks like they're going to be here for a while."

"Okay, wait a minute," Locco called out. He walked back into the yard, grabbed the bag then hurried over to the car. He got inside, looking at Willow admirably. She put that Cutti in reverse and started backing down the alley when a couple of policemen came out of the back of Anthony's house and flashed his light on them.

"Hey!" shouted one of the policemen. "Stop!" Willow stared at them for a second then looked over at Locco.

"Stop and put the car in park, and I'll take care of it," Locco assured her. He hit a button on his phone, typed something, and pressed send. The two officers walked toward the car, one black and the other Mexican, looking at them suspiciously. They shined their lights at the plates and then scaled it up to the windshield right on both of them.

"Where are you coming from?" asked the black officer.

"We're just coming from my cousin's house, and he lives right there," said Locco, pointing. "He was working on my car, but when we heard gunshots, we went into the house. My baby out here visiting from Georgia, and I ain't trying to have her family mad at me." The cop shined his light down on Willow, and she looked at him seductively. Her titties were already sitting up to her shoulders, and she straightened her posture suggestively.

"How you doin'?" asked Willow in a southern drawl.

"What part of Georgia are you from?" the Mexican officer questioned.

"I'm from Savannah, Georgia," Willow replied. She leaned down and looked at the officer standing outside of Locco's door. His cousin walked out of the backyard, and it distracted the cops.

"Stop right there," said the black officer, placing his hand on the handle of his gun.

"My fault," said Locco's cousin. "I was coming out to see what was going on. I thought they were gone, but I see y'all got them hemmed up."

"You know them?" asked the Mexican officer.

"Yeah! That's my cousin Diablo and his friend visiting from out of town," his cousin explained. The officers looked at one another for a second then the Black one looked down at Willow.

"Enjoy your visit," said the Black cop, smiling.

"You need to take her to a nicer part of California, bro," said the Mexican officer. "You got her in the hood and shit while murders are occurring around y'all!"

"Yes, sir," Locco agreed, laughing. "We about to get the fuck from over here right now! Good night, officers!"

"Good night, officers," Willow added, laughing.

****

"Why you come get me?" asked JD, climbing off the back of the bike.

"Wait a minute," said Yusuf, pulling out his phone. He pressed a few things and put the phone up to his ear. "Hello? Okay." Yusuf held the phone out to JD and looked at him smugly.

"Who is that?" JD spat, frowning.

"Get the phone, boy!" Yusuf scoffed. JD snatched it out of his hand and put it to his ear.

"Hello," JD snapped.

"What do you want, nigga?" snapped Willow, sounding annoyed. JD looked at his uncle in confusion.

"How the fuck did you find her?" uttered JD curiously. "Wait… don't answer that. I want to talk to my Lil' Baby first. Where the fuck you been? I've been calling yo' fuckin' phone, and yo' ass ain't answered not once!" JD fussed.

"Oh… so now you give a fuck about a bitch?" Willow scoffed. "I left my phone in Shaggy's car. It's so nice to know that you give a fuck now." The tone in her voice was so dry that even water couldn't moisten it up.

"Whose phone are you on?" JD asked curiously.

"I'm on Shaggy's brother's phone," Willow explained. "He said your uncle Yusuf called to see if he could locate me, and I just so happen to be with him."

"Who the fuck is *he*, and what the fuck you doin' wit' that nigga?" JD snapped angrily. "Yo' ass ain't out there bein' a hoe, are you?"

"Who the fuck you talkin' to, nigga! I can't believe you just said that shit to me, JD! I'm fuckin' pregnant by you, so why would you think that I'm out here being a hoe?" Willow retorted. "I was actually happy as fuck when Locco told me that you were going to call me on his phone, but now I feel like I was better off only worrying!" JD didn't say anything for a second because he realized he was overreacting.

"I'm just pissed that yo' ass ain't have yo' phone on you. It's bad enough yo' ass ran to California to that nigga Cypher, but then you hang the fuck up on me when you carrying my baby!"

"For your information, nigga, I ain't even with that bitch made nigga! He tried to jump on me," Willow retorted, amped. "I told that nigga that my baby ain't his, and he flipped the fuck out on me!"

"What!" JD shouted furiously. "On my mama, I'm on my way out there! Soon as we get off the phone, I'm booking the next flight out to that muthafucka!"

"Nigga, stop fakin'." Willow chuckled. "You know yo' ass ain't coming no fucking where. If you really gave a fuck, then you would have come and got me the other night!"

"Don't you start that shit, Lil' Baby!" JD fussed. "I fucked up, okay! Would you just let that shit go and forgive me already, damn!" Willow was getting a kick out of hearing JD frustrated, but she did miss the fuck out of him and wanted to be with him even more.

"I guess I can let the shit go," Willow conceded with a big smile on her face. "Where the fuck you at since you're putting down a fucking interrogation?"

"I'm still down at my cabin in the Ozarks," JD explained. "I still say yo' ass should have known where the fuck I was coming because I've always told you that when shit gets hectic we're heading down here." Willow realized that she had fucked up too because he did constantly tell her that the hideout was in the Ozarks.

"I don't know, JD. Things were so crazy and hectic that I panicked. I just thought about getting as far away from St. Louis as possible, and Cali seemed like the ideal place to go. You should have come and got me or told me where to go since you're the head of this relationship. The man is supposed to be the lead, and you know a bitch knows how to follow instructions. Shit, I was controlled by O'Bannon for years! Ain't that what you told me when we agreed to be together? You're the man, so you're the head of the household?" Willow reminded him.

"Yeah, I said that, but…"

"But got fucked, nigga! And right now, I'm not even concerned with the bullshit anymore. Right now, the only thing important to me is getting back to you, and all I need for you to do is send me the address so I can GPS your location and navigate to you when I touch down at the airport." A slight smile crept on JD's face because Willow's words were like music to his ears.

"I miss the fuck out of you, Lil' Baby," JD professed. "My dick's been aching to feel them tight ass walls in between your legs."

"Is that all you miss, nigga... my pussy?" Willow asked with a hint of an attitude.

"Stop playing with me, Lil' Baby! I miss yo' ugly ass being in my arms every night when I go to sleep and waking up in the morning without you is killing me!" A tingling sensation danced in between her legs, and a satisfied smile came across her face.

"I miss the shit out of you too, Big Baby," Willow admitted then sighed. "I haven't had a decent night's sleep either, but I want you to know that I'm gon' slap the shit out of you when I see you, though."

"Don't get beside yourself now, Willow," JD reminded her. "'Cause yo' ass ain't gone slap shit right here!"

"All right. We gon' see," she replied. "My fuckin' hand is itchin' and twitchin' like a muthafucka too!" She laughed to let him know she was joking, and he relaxed a bit because he knew that Willow is a woman of her word.

"How my baby doing inside your belly?" asked JD, sounding concerned. "Yo' ass been eating vegetables?"

"Yes, but I haven't been able to keep shit down, though!"

"You got morning sickness, huh?"

"Yes, but everyone keeps saying it will pass," Willow whined. JD heard someone talking in the background, and he wondered who she was around. "JD, I need to give Locco back his phone, so he can take care of some business. I love you with all my heart and soul, and I would never betray you or our trust, so don't ever think that I'm out here with some nigga being disrespectful. You know I'm a loyal bitch!"

"Yo' ass betta not be! I'm not fuckin' playin' with you either, Lil' Baby! I love you with all of my heart and soul too. I want you to know that I will kill you, that nigga, and his family if I think you've been out there fuckin' around on me!"

Willow giggled because she knew he was serious, and she loved it!

"Boy, bye!" *Click.* Willow laughed because she'd hung up on him again before he could say something slick to her.

Zzzzzzzzzzzz! Zzzzzzzzzzzzz! The phone vibrated, and Willow looked at it.

"Hello," she said cockily.

"I'm gone beat yo' ass for real, Willow!" declared JD, sounding frustrated as hell. "I love you, Lil' Baby."

"I love you too, JD," Willow replied and hung up the phone. She looked up at Locco then handed it to him.

"I'll be over here tomorrow with a car for you. I don't know if I like the idea of you driving all that way by yourself," said Locco. "I appreciate what you did for me, and it won't go unrewarded."

"Thank you for your concern, and I appreciate all the love, but I'm leaving tomorrow," Willow assured him. "I have to get back to my candy daddy, especially since I killed three niggas up here fucking around with you. I told him that I'd be flying just in case the police are listening. O'Bannon got them connections, and I don't put shit past that nigga!" Locco looked down at her with his eyebrow raised then he laughed.

"You ain't got shit to worry about, ma, because no one knows who you are in Cali. Also, if you need me to go holla at that nigga, O'Bannon, I'll make a special trip to the Lou just to handle that lightweight for you! I owe you that!" Locco assured her. "When we were driving away, I thought about something. The scene looked like a robbery, so we should be in the clear. I sent my cousin around there to pick up my truck, and he gon' bring it to me tomorrow."

"That's what's up," said Willow nonchalantly. "But I'm still leaving."

"It's all good, Willow. I'll be here in the morning to drop everything off to you," Locco replied and smiled. "And thank you for saving my ass! I probably would have been the one laid up in there dead if you didn't handle that shit. That nigga, Anthony, had been down with me for a very long time, and I'm fucked up about him crossing me."

"I guess it goes to show you that money is the root to all evil. The nigga you thought was down for you had crossed you out, and it took a bitch from the Lou to come in and save the day. It's all in a day's work for a gangsta like me," Willow boasted arrogantly.

"I guess so, lil' ma, 'cause you're the fuckin' truth!"

CHAPTER FOURTEEN

"*You* need to be quiet 'cause Willow is in there sleep," Shaggy whispered, feeling agitated.

"I promise I won't make any noise," Duke assured him, tiptoeing toward Shaggy's room. "It was too late to drive all the way home from the studio, and my wife understood." Shaggy followed him into his bedroom and shut the door. "Besides, I really wanted to see you!"

"I've missed you too, but I'm tired as fuck! Locco and Willow had left the club, and he just brought her back to the house."

"Where were they? I know she ain't fucking with your brother now, is she?" asked Duke nosily. "She was just with Cypher, and their shit went left. This might drive him over the edge, and I don't know what that shit looks like!"

"Chile, please! Willow ain't stunting Locco or Cypher. She's pregnant by JD and has plans on marrying him when she gets back to St. Louis," Shaggy scoffed. "Cypher tried to attack her because she told him the exact same thing."

"That's why he sounded out of it when I called him earlier," Duke made mention.

"That nigga's balls probably still hurt," said Shaggy, laughing.

"Willow said she tried to kick them into his stomach when he put his hands on her."

"I hope you didn't get in the middle of that shit," Duke frowned.

"I ain't worried about Cypher. We're back in California, and I'll have Locco beat the shit out of him. Please believe me!" Duke looked at Shaggy and laughed. He took his sweatshirt off and threw it on the floor next to the bed. Next, he walked up to Shaggy and pulled the belt on his robe loose.

"We can fool around a little bit, can't we?" Duke asked lustfully. Shaggy looked back toward the door then back at Duke.

"I guess we can a little bit," Shaggy replied, smiling shyly.

"Good," said Duke, dropping to his knees. "'Cause I've missed you terribly!"

****

Shaggy was passed out after his lustful romp in the bed with Duke. He had so much built up pressure inside that it felt good to have Duke come over to get the lead out. However, there was an ulterior motive to Duke's actions. He came over to scope out Willow's situation in hopes that she would make it easy for him to get her back to St. Louis.

Duke pulled his arm from up under Shaggy and watched as he turned over and nestled against his pillow. He slowly got up off of the bed and walked around to Shaggy's side to grab his phone. Duke slid open the screen and looked at the text messages to see if Cypher had contacted him about Willow. Duke wasn't getting anywhere with it, but an interesting text from Locco came through while he was snooping. It said something about being there in two hours to give Willow the car to drive back to St.

Louis. Duke thought it was good that Willow was leaving, but he knew she wasn't going back to O'Bannon. There was so much pressure on him to bring Willow back, and the $300,000 that was promised to him upon delivery made things sweeter. Duke figured if there was some way he could convince Willow to let him ride back with her. It would give him some time to formulate a plan to get her to O'Bannon.

Several Hours Later

"Did you have company last night 'cause I heard some bumping and moaning through the walls?" Willow asked, packing her toiletries into her bag. Shaggy looked at her and smiled.

"I had a little something, something going on, but I hope we weren't too loud," Shaggy apologized bashfully.

"It didn't disturb me," Willow admitted. "I had gotten up to go to the bathroom, and that's when I heard it. You must have been putting on your best porn star performance because all I kept hearing was 'Oh, Shaggy'!" Willow giggled and placed her bag down on the floor.

"It had been a minute since I've seen Duke, so he was..." Shaggy realized he let the cat out of the bag, and a look of embarrassment came across his face.

"Baby, I am not here to judge!" Willow assured him. "I don't think he's worth your time, and you could do so much better, but we can't help who we love."

"This is so true," Shaggy admitted. "I'm just glad you realized it and kicked Cypher's ass to the curb. You got to meet the real deal yesterday, and my brother seems to be smitten with you!"

"That's because I saved that nigga's life," Willow scoffed. "I was only supposed to be going to get my phone out of your car and ended up on a whole excursion with Locco's ass!"

"That's how his ass rolls. That's why I don't like riding somewhere with him," Shaggy confessed. "One time, he had me dress up in drag to ride somewhere with him. We ended up making a drug run, and I was pissed off 'cause the men he was meeting with tried to get on me!" Willow laughed.

"You shouldn't be so cute!" Willow gushed.

"Why thank you, sweetie!" Shaggy gushed back. The doorbell rang, and they both looked at each other. "That's probably Locco at the door." Shaggy turned and walked over to the door then opened it up without asking who it was. A surprised look came across his face when Cypher was standing in front of him looking worn down and crazy.

"Willow! I need to talk to you!" Cypher demanded. "I'm sorry for being an asshole, and I think we can work it out! I don't give a fuck about you being pregnant by that other nigga! I can offer you a lot more and will treat you like a princess!"

"My nigga treats me like a queen, so I'm not interested in shit you're selling, Cypher! Why don't you go find Indigo's ass and profess your love for her! I don't give a fuck about you or your feelings!" Willow spat vehemently.

"Why are you doing this to me!" Cypher whined uncontrollably.

"Boy! You're doing this to yourself," Shaggy interjected, frowning. "And you stink! You smell like a distillery!"

"Shut the fuck up, Shaggy, and let me in this muthafucka!" Cypher demanded, trying to push through the door. Willow reached down into her purse and pulled out the gun she had gotten from Locco.

"Let the muthafucka in," said Willow confidently. "I got this here hammer, and I have no problems putting a slug in his bitch ass if he tries anything."

"You and Locco ain't gone worry me," said Shaggy, moving out of the way. Cypher fell through the door and looked at Shaggy with an evil grimace on his face. "I don't give a fuck about you looking at me like that! Willow's got my back, and I know she'll fuck you up for me!"

"I surely will," Willow confirmed.

Cypher walked further into the apartment and stopped in the middle of the living room when he realized Willow was holding a gun. She placed it up under her arm and stared at Cypher with a mean look on her face. He had plans on trying to force Willow to come with him, but after he saw that she was packing, he knew that trying to deebo her wasn't going to work.

"Why do you have a gun?" Cypher asked nervously. "And where did you get it from?"

"That's none of your fuckin' business. What do you want?" Willow asked firmly.

"I can't believe you're so hostile toward the man who absolutely loves you the most!" Cypher declared. "I haven't been able to sleep, and all of my thoughts have been consumed with thoughts of you!"

"Sounds like a personal problem to me," Willow replied smugly. Shaggy laughed at Willow's response, and Cypher didn't feel too happy about it.

"Why are you being such a bitch, Willow? You loved this dick when it was all in your mouth, so what gives? Why have you switched up on me?" Cypher questioned, feeling perplexed.

"You really want to know?" asked Willow, smiling. "I had a false, preconceived notion that we were from the same world. Your music made you sound like this larger than life gangsta that handled business and didn't give a fuck about what others thought," Willow explained. "What I found out was the fact that you're a bitch ass nigga! You're trying to mirror a man who I found out was a solid ass nigga. You could never be like Locco even if you tried!"

"Did I hear my name?" asked Locco, walking through the door. Everyone turned to look at him except Willow because she was facing the entrance. "I love being the topic of conversation. What are we talking about?"

"I was just telling Cypher that I met you, and he could never be like you in a million years," Willow explained. Locco looked over at Cypher and smiled.

"Leave cuz alone," Locco suggested and chuckled. "I'm glad the lil nigga idolizes me, and we should celebrate him for putting us on in the music industry." Cypher looked at his cousin, and cut his eyes.

"Nigga, did you fuck her?" Cypher yelled vehemently.

"What?" Locco asked with a confused look on his face. "Are you serious right now? I mean... are you really being serious right now?"

"I'm serious as cancer!" Cypher retorted. "What the fuck is you doing over here?"

"You better watch how you're talking to me, nigga," Locco advised

Cypher. "You know I'll knock your punk ass out! I owe you anyway for putting your hands on Shaggy." Cypher didn't look phased by Locco's threats.

"Fuck this nigga," Willow spat. "Do you have everything for me?"

"I do. Are you ready?" Locco asked, staring at her.

"Most definitely!" Willow replied.

"What the fuck y'all talking about?" Cypher asked angrily.

"None of your fuckin' business," Willow replied while she leaned down and picked up her bag. She put it on one shoulder and walked over to Shaggy. She hugged him tightly because she was appreciative for all of his help. "Thank you for being so wonderfully awesome!"

"Chile! I didn't know you knew the word awesome!" Shaggy joked as he giggled uncontrollably. "I just thought you knew muthafucka, bitch, bitch ass nigga, and fuck!" He continued to laugh as Willow walked into his arms again. They squeezed each other tightly then let go.

"You'll have to come visit me, Shaggy, especially after I have the baby," Willow mentioned.

"That sounds like a plan!" Shaggy replied happily.

"Come on, Locco. I'm ready," Willow announced as she picked up her purse. Cypher pushed passed Shaggy and grabbed Willow by the arm. She looked at him angrily then put the gun she was holding up to the side of his head. "Get yo' muthafuckin' hands off of me before I blow your brains out all over Shaggy's apartment!"

"I'm already dead," Cypher uttered pitifully. "I need you in my life, Willow, and I can't live without you!"

"Is this nigga serious?" asked Locco in disbelief. "I know the nigga who said he don't need a bitch for shit but to keep his dick warm ain't over here crying about a bitch!" Willow lifted an eyebrow at Locco.

"I ain't just some bitch," Willow replied sarcastically. "This nigga ain't never had good pussy from a real savage, and my juicy got him going crazy!"

"It's not all about that, Willow! You are my soulmate, and I realized that I fucked up royally! Can we please just try to start over?" Cypher begged.

"I'm over this shit, and I'm going home to my man," Willow declared. "Now get the fuck out of my way or else you're going to be deeply saddened by the outcome!" Cypher saw the seriousness in Willow's eyes and knew that she would shoot the shit out of him if he didn't move. He leaned in and kissed her forehead sadly.

"I'm sorry, Willow, for my behavior," Cypher apologized. "I hope there's some way we can be friends."

"Maybe, but right now, I'm not interested. So, have a nice life, Cypher," Willow replied. She pulled her arm away from him and left Shaggy's house with Locco following her. She was surprised by the way Cypher was handling the situation, but sometimes people don't respond the way you think they should, and that's life.

CHAPTER FIFTEEN

*W*illow called JD and told him she was on her way to him. He was happy, but he didn't like the fact that she was riding by herself. They talked on the phone for a while, but Willow wanted to concentrate on the road. She promised that she would call him in an hour when she scheduled herself a bathroom break.

"What you doing up so early?" asked Yusuf, walking onto porch.

"I've been on the phone with Willow," JD replied. "She's on the highway on her way here."

"Is she by herself or did someone go with her?" asked Yusuf. "And I thought you said she was flying to Missouri."

"Apparently, she changed her mind. She's by herself, but Locco gave her a gun and an extra clip in case she needed it," JD replied. "I wanted her to wait, and I was gone fly out so we can ride back together, but she didn't want to do it that way."

"It sounds like she's a bit stubborn like you," Yusuf chuckled. JD looked at him and smirked.

"I think Lil' Baby's got me beat, but I can give her a run for her money," JD admitted. "I even took the time out to say a prayer for safe passage."

"That's good," Yusuf replied. "A man should pray for his woman daily in order to uplift her, and ask Allah for her protection." JD shook his head at his uncle and walked into the house. A car turned into the gated yard and headed toward the house. Yusuf narrowed his eyes for a second to see if he could recognize the automobile then realized it were Sister Sarah, and someone else coming down the road. Yusuf looked back at the door then came down the steps to greet them.

The car pulled up, and Sister Sarah turned it sideways to make it easy to pull back off. Yusuf noticed that Yanni was in the car, and she looked quite excited. There was a big smile on her face, and she quickly exited out of the vehicle and ran around to Yusuf.

"Yusuf! I have wonderful news!" Yanni shouted.

"Hey, Yanni." Yusuf smiled as she ran up to him. "What brings you over?"

"I've met my one-year sober mark!" she shouted excitedly.

"Isn't that wonderful?" Sister Sarah added, getting out of the car. She had on a mini skirt with a tight-fitting t-shirt, and Yusuf lustfully looked at her with a dirty smile on his face when he noticed her nipples straining against the cotton fabric.

"It is Sister Sarah," Yusuf replied happily. He moved Yanni out of the way and walked up to Sister Sarah. "Can I give you a hug?"

"Sure," Sister Sarah agreed. She laughed as Yusuf wrapped his arms around her, and pulled her as close to him as physically possible. He placed his hands against her back and then slid them down to her butt, gripping it. "Oh!" she quipped.

"My fault... sorry!" Yusuf apologized. He put his hands around her waist and hugged her again blissfully.

"Damn, Unc! I didn't know you had bitches!" JD yelled walking onto the porch. Yanni's back was to JD, and her eyes widened when she recognized his voice.

"JD," Yanni uttered, turning around to face him. "My beautiful son!" A big smile was on her face, but JD's expression didn't match hers at all.

"Where the fuck did you come from?" JD snapped angrily.

"Is that any way to talk to your mother!" yelled Yanni, feeling offended.

"Bitch, I don't know who the fuck you are!" JD replied sarcastically. "The last time I saw my mama, she was a strung-out crack hoe that was sucking dick for a five-dollar hit."

"Come on, JD," Yusuf scoffed. "Your mother has been working very hard to stay sober. Today is her one-year anniversary of sobriety!"

"I don't give a fuck," JD snapped. "This bitch ran off and didn't look back not once! I'm fuckin' twenty-four years old now, and it's been three years since I've seen this hoe! Do you really think I give a fuck about her being sober for a year? She was high basically all of my fucking life; at least as long as I can remember!"

"I understand that you're upset with me, Julio... and what I did to you was unforgivable, but I was sick. I had a problem, baby, but I want you to understand that I love you! My soul has ached, and I constantly beat myself up for what I've done to you! Yanni confessed full of conviction.

"I don't want to hear that shit!" JD scoffed. "You knew where the fuck I was, and you didn't once reach out to me! If you didn't know where the fuck I was then I could understand, but my granny certainly knew, and you knew how to get in touch with her!"

"I think both of you should stop and take a deep breath," Sister Sarah suggested. "Let's refocus ourselves, and try not to blame each other for mistakes that were made in the past."

"Who the fuck is you?" JD spat. "This ain't no fuckin' therapy session, and I don't need to take a fuckin' breath, so what you need to do is mind your own fuckin' business before I hurt yo' muthafuckin' feelings!"

"JD, don't talk to her like that!" Yusuf demanded with a frown on his face. "She's a nun, and you need to show her some respect!" JD looked at Sister Sarah and rolled his eyes.

"She ain't dressed like no nun. She's dressed like a hoe!" JD replied, frowning. Yanni looked at him with disappointment on her face, and for some reason, it made him feel bad. "My fault, ma'am," JD apologized. "But fuck you, Yanni!" JD turned and walked toward the house.

"Well fuck you too, Julio Delgado! You ain't nothing special, black ass nigga, and if you can't forgive me, then you ain't no better than me!" Yanni yelled. "I was a fucked up individual, and I apologize for being a horrible mother! I'm sorry that crack meant more to me than you! I'm only human, and everyone falls short sometime in their lives!" JD stopped mid-stride and turned around.

"Do you know that I just moved all of your shit to the basement a few months ago," JD replied. "I used to go to the downstairs apartment where I put your shit and just sit there wondering about what the fuck happened to you. I didn't know if your ass was dead or alive, and all I remember is Willow saying that 'God takes care of fools and babies, so you and your mother should be alright.'"

"Julio, can we please have a civilized conversation without you cursing at me? I have changed... really, I have, and I want us to be able to put the past behind us and move on with the healing process," Yanni begged. She looked back at Yusuf humbly. "I made amends with Yusuf, and he's helped so much with my sobriety. I love you son, and I want to be a part of your life, so we can be a family again."

"I got my own family," JD retorted. "Willow's on her way here now, and she's pregnant with my baby. We're going to get married, and that's all I need to get by."

"Quit being selfish got damnit!" Yusuf demanded. "You act like people aren't allowed to make fucking mistakes! You gave me a second chance and put me up in this house. You had a lot of anger and resentment toward me that still comes out from time to time, but we're working through it! Give your mother a chance, please, for all of our sakes. Maybe she can be a better grandmother to your unborn child than she was a mother to you!" JD stared angrily at his uncle, but his face softened a bit because on the low he was happy to see his mother looking healthy and beautiful. He was the spitting image of her, and they both had smooth dark ebony colored skin. She'd put on some weight, and her hair flowed down her back wildly.

"Please give me a chance, BooBoo," Yanni stammered. She called him by the nickname she'd given him as a baby. It made JD feel some type of way because it had been years since anyone had called him that. "I can't say sorry enough, son, but I promise I will try my best to show you in order to make things right between us." She walked toward JD with tears flowing down her cheeks. "I promise that I won't ever leave you or turn my back on you again." She stopped in front of JD with her eyes filled with tears. "Set your soul free, and forgive me." She held out her arms in front of her as tears rushed down her face. JD stared at her with an indifferent look on his face then he walked into her arms and hugged her tightly.

"I'm still mad at you," he mumbled. "But I guess we can work on that."

"Most definitely, son," Yanni sobbed. "Most definitely!"

"I was just about to prepare us some lunch," Yusuf announced. "Why don't we go inside, Sister Sarah, and give the two of them some time to talk."

"I think that's an excellent idea," Sister Sarah replied. "Lead the way."

Yusuf grabbed Sister Sarah by the hand, and they went into the house while JD and Yanni made themselves comfortable on the porch.

"Sister Sarah, how long have you been a nun?" asked Yusuf being nosy.

"I'm really not a nun," she replied. "They call me Sister Sarah because I've always preached black power, even though I was a drug addict. I came to the farm when my life had hit rock bottom. Like Yanni, I was strung out too, but luckily I didn't have any children."

"I thought you were a woman of the cloth. I bet you were

something else when you was getting high, weren't you?" Yusuf gloated.

"To say the least," she replied. "We all make mistakes in life, but it's how we correct those mistakes that tells a lot about one's character."

"I agree," Yusuf chimed. He looked behind him, staring at JD and Yanni on the porch talking. "I totally agree."

CHAPTER SIXTEEN

*W*illow had been on the road for about fifteen hours, and her body was starting to shut down. She'd made a few stops to use the bathroom and get gas, but it appeared that those breaks weren't long enough. She decided to stop at a motel in order to take a shower, eat, and get some rest. She talked with Keena and JD a few times throughout the day, and couldn't wait until she was safely in their presence.

Willow pulled into a motel parking lot off Highway 50 in Colorado. There was a restaurant up the road that looked appetizing, and she could smell the fumes from their exhaust in the air. *A greasy hamburger with some fries smothered in cheese would be so good right now,* she thought. Willow chuckled at what JD would say to her if he saw her eating it. She went into the office to grab herself a room, but little did she know, someone else would be checking in also.

"Thanks, Craig, for doing this," said Duke, grabbing his bag out of the back.

"You didn't tell me we would be coming all the way to Colorado," Craig complained. "This is a long fucking way!"

"I know, and I got you, man," Duke assured him. "Here, take this cash, and go get us a room with two beds. You can leave in the morning, and I'll give you the cash I promised."

"How about you give me the cash now, and I'll take my chances on the road," Craig frowned.

"Can you at least go and get me a room?" Duke begged. "I've seemed to have left my identification in California." Craig glared at him then opened his car door.

"I'll be back," Craig scoffed. He got out of the car and walked toward the office. Duke noticed Willow coming out, so he slid down in the seat so she couldn't see him. He watched as she went to her car and got out her bag. Next, she went up the stairs and opened the door to her room. Duke was pleased that everything was going well, and his plan to take Willow in the morning will hopefully go as well as things did today. Craig came back out of the office and headed toward the car. He was ready to part ways with Duke because he had a sneaking suspicion that Duke was on some bullshit, and he didn't want to be a part of any of it!

Craig opened his car door and climbed inside. He reached out and handed Duke the key then held his hand out to be paid. A smug smile spread across Duke's face before he reached inside of his bag and pulled out a stack of $100 bills.

"Here you go, Craig, $2,000 like we discussed," said Duke, placing the money in his hand.

"I should charge you extra because I didn't know we would be coming this far," Craig complained. Duke reached back inside his bag and pulled out a few more bills. "Here's $3,000 more, Craig; you've earned it. However, please, remember that you weren't with me, and you didn't drop me off."

"No problem," said Craig, counting his money. "Don't fuck up the hotel room either!"

"I won't," Duke assured him. "I'm just going to grab something to eat and get some rest. My friend should be here to get me in the morning."

Duke shook Craig's hand and exited the car. He looked up at Willow's room number then looked at the key Craig had given him. Duke's room was located on the bottom floor, and it just so happened to be in front of Willow's car. This would make it easy for him to nab her because he wouldn't have to go far. It's like taking candy from a baby!

Willow woke up the next morning feeling slightly refreshed. She talked to JD into the wee hours of the night because she didn't like being in the worn-down motel by herself. They were FaceTiming, so he was able to see the shabby accommodations and get a better understanding of where she was staying. He wanted to catch a flight out to meet her, but Willow insisted on him staying put. He told her about his plan of action when they got home. He was ready to get married and running really wasn't in his blood. JD told Willow that he was still angry with her, but a huge part of him was happy to know that she was safe and doing all right.

Willow walked out of the room and headed toward her car. She had grabbed some donuts from the diner last night when she bought her dinner so that she wouldn't have to make any stops not unless she had to go to the bathroom. She walked up to the back door and hit the locks. She grabbed the handle and opened it up then swung her bag around to place it on the seat. She leaned down then suddenly felt a pain in the back of head, and everything went black.

Duke looked around to see if anyone saw what he had done. Next, he pushed Willow into the back seat and took the keys out of her hand. He closed the door behind her and expediently climbed into the driver's seat. He started the car and peeled out of the parking lot headed toward the interstate. He was excited that everything had gone as planned, and they'd be in St. Louis by nightfall with a big payday waiting for him.

****

JD woke up in a cold sweat because he had a dream that Willow had gotten into a car accident. He nervously looked around the room trying to figure out his surroundings. It took a second before he gained his faculties and was able to rationally remember that it was just a dream. He grabbed his phone off of the nightstand and instantly dialed Willow's number. The phone went straight to voicemail, and it seemed to be a mistake. JD dialed the number again, but the same thing happened. He went to her Snap, Facebook, and Instagram, but she hadn't made any posts since she went out of town. JD was starting to feel nervous, but he knew that he might be overreacting. He laid back against the pillows and sat his phone on top of his chest. He planned on calling Willow again in a few hours, and she'd better answer the damn phone.

****

"I got your package, and I'm headed to St. Louis," Duke boasted proudly. "I was shockingly surprised that it was so easy to get her. It was like taking candy from a baby."

"She didn't try to fight you?" O'Bannon asked, surprised.

"Nope. I caught her by surprise," Duke replied, amused. "She's knocked out in the back seat. I made sure that I went through her bag, and I took her phone. She even had a gun on her, and I took that too." O'Bannon smiled because it didn't surprise him that, even in the middle of nowhere, Willow had a strap.

"When do you expect to be here?" O'Bannon asked curiously. "I need to make preparations and figure out where to keep her."

"You should have had all that shit planned out when you asked me to take her," Duke complained. "Just figure something out!" Duke didn't want to hear anything else, and he hung up the phone pissed. He couldn't believe that he was just flying by the seat of his pants and had to wait to find out the rest of the plan.

Willow was lying in the back seat and started to come to. The back of her head was pounding, and she could hear someone talking. It was obvious she was in a moving car, but she had no idea what was going on. She sat up in the seat and noticed it was Duke that was driving.

"What the fuck!" shouted Willow? "Ouch!" She rubbed her head because it was steady pounding. "Why did you hit me in my fucking head?"

"Let me call you back," Duke uttered. He was talking to Shaggy on the phone but didn't tell him what he'd done. He hung up his phone and stared at her in the rearview mirror. "Sorry about that, Willow. I didn't know what else to do."

"You could have just pulled a gun out on me like any respectable criminal would have done," Willow complained.

"That might be the problem 'cause I'm not a criminal," Duke replied.

"I can't tell," Willow scoffed. "Cause the shit you're doing right now is criminal activity."

"I'm just taking you to O'Bannon so you can be prosecuted for the crimes you've committed against him. Let's just call it a citizen's arrest."

"I ain't done shit to O'Bannon! So, I guess he wants me to tell about how he tried to shoot JD in the head from behind. What I did was self-defense, and it's not a crime when you prevent a person from killing the man you love! They'll just give me vehicular assault or something. I should have ran over his ass after I hit him!"

"You are one mean woman. Has anyone ever told you that?" asked Duke, frowning. "Why are you so violent?"

"Because muthafuckas make me violent," Willow complained. "Where are we, and how long have I been out?"

"We're almost at the Colorado border and about to cross over into Kansas," Duke explained. "We've been on the road for about three hours, and I must say we've been making good timing."

"This is so fucked up, Duke," Willow scoffed. "I already didn't like you, and you've made things worse." Duke laughed.

"You can't kill me with kindness, Willow," he replied. "And before you go looking, I took all of your weapons out of your purse." Willow glared at him as she looked inside her bag.

"Fucker!" Willow mumbled. They rode in silence for a few minutes. "Can we pull over? I really have to go to the bathroom, and I think my breakfast is ready to come up."

"You can't hold it until the next rest stop?" Duke whined.

"No! I'm fucking pregnant," she complained.

"That's right. I forgot," Duke replied. "I wonder what O'Bannon's going to do since you're pregnant. Knowing his ignorant ass, he'll probably pay for you an abortion."

"There's no fucking way I'm getting an abortion. O'Bannon's got me completely fucked up!" She frowned. "He just better hope that I don't kill his ass, because if I don't, then JD will definitely make sure it happens along with your stupid ass!"

"Well, I guess we'll have to see what happens now won't we," Duke announced. "Now, sit back and shut up while I pull into this rest stop."

CHAPTER SEVENTEEN

*D*uke pulled off the road headed toward the rest stop when he saw two highway patrol cars parked outside the area. A nervous feeling came across him, and he almost kept going. Willow noticed his apprehension and figured she could use this situation to her advantage.

"I hope you don't think you can keep driving," Willow scoffed. "My stomach is cramping, and I really need to go."

"I don't trust you with those police sitting right there." Duke frowned. "Your ass might try to be slick and get away."

"I ain't trying to be shit. I have to use the bathroom," Willow replied. "Also, the way I see it, I'm getting a free ride home, and I don't have to do any of the driving. I can sit my ass in this back seat and ride in comfort." Duke glared at her through the rearview.

"You got it all figured out, huh?" Duke snapped. "You better not try to be slick or I'm gone hit your ass across the head again, and knock you out!" Willow looked at him and frowned.

"Just pull the fuck over so I can go take a piss!" Willow snapped.

Duke pulled the car over and came to a complete stop. Willow hopped out of the back and took off running toward the bathroom. Duke nervously exited the car and made his way over to a picnic table that sat by the building. The police officers looked at him strangely, and Duke put a stupid smirk on his face.

"My wife had to pee really bad," Duke explained. "She's only a few months pregnant, and it seems like we have to stop every twenty minutes for her to pee."

"I've experienced that before," said one of the officers. "You might want to consider flying next time." Duke laughed. "Where are you on your way to?"

"Chicago," Duke replied. "My mother-in-law lives there, and we're going to visit. We recently moved to Phoenix, Arizona for work, and my wife is feeling homesick." The officer that wasn't doing much talking took a look at the car. He looked over at Duke then mumbled something to the other officer. "How much of the highway do you guys cover?" asked Duke curiously.

"We cover up to the Kansas border and about six counties in Colorado," the officer replied. The other officer walked off toward his cruiser, and Willow came walking from the bathroom.

"I'm ready to go." Willow growled. "And I want to stop off to get something to eat when we are close to a restaurant." Duke smiled at Willow.

"Is there anything else, dear?" he asked. Willow looked at him and cut her eyes.

"No comment," she scoffed and got into the back seat.

"Women…you can't live with them, and you can't live without them." Duke laughed. He walked off and went to get into the car. He nervously watched the policeman who was sitting in his cruiser.

"Why yo' ass looking nervous?" asked Willow, lifting an eyebrow. "You scared that I'm gone get yo' ass caught up?"

"That never crossed my mind." Duke smiled.

"I'm sure," Willow replied. "I'm gone have something even better for that ass. I don't play with the police, and I definitely don't fight fair."

"Those are things that are not surprising to me," Duke replied. "Just continue to act normal, and I won't have to put a bullet in you."

"Yo' weak ass won't do no shit like that." Willow laughed. "You know O'Bannon would beat the shit out of you if you harm a hair on my head."

"I don't know about that," Duke replied. "He's pretty pissed at you right now." Duke's phone began to ring. "Speaking of the devil." Willow looked at him vehemently.

"Oh yeah! Tell that bitch ass nigga that I'm gone finish what I started," Willow murmured.

"You can tell him that yourself. Hello," said Duke, sounding amused.

"What's your location?" O'Bannon demanded. "I haven't received a phone call, so I was wondering what was going on."

"We're just outside of Kansas. Willow had to pee, so we stopped at a rest stop," Duke explained.

"Don't worry about where the fuck we at!" shouted Willow. "Just know, bitch ass nigga, that I got something for you!"

"Put her on the phone," O'Bannon ordered.

"Sure thing," Duke replied. "Here, O'Bannon wants to talk to you." Willow snatched the phone out of his hand.

"What the fuck you want?" Willow snapped.

"Did you honestly think that I couldn't touch you?" he asked confidently. "Running to California wasn't the best course of action, and when Duke brings you back to St. Louis, I got something for you."

"I got something for yo ass too," Willow replied. "And I guarantee yo ass ain't gon' like it!"

"Willow, why are you so hostile towards me? I love you more than life itself. I've provided a wonderful life for you. I spoiled you with clothes, jewelry, and an extensive sneaker collection… I was even about to buy you a house over in the Central West End."

"I don't give a fuck about none of that shit! You tried to control my life, and that's where you had me fucked up! I'm pregnant with JD's baby, and we're getting married as soon as I get up out of this jam. What you better hope, bitch ass nigga, is that I don't make it to St. Louis with this guy. If I do, it's going to be the death of the both of you!" Willow hung up the phone and let down the window. She threw it out on the highway, and she watched the car behind them run over it.

"What the fuck did you do that for?" shouted Duke. "Why didn't my dumb ass lock the fucking windows?"

"Cause you a dumb muthafucka!" Willow laughed. "I'm about to go to sleep, so fuck O'Bannon, and fuck you too!" Willow lifted up her bag and adjusted it on the seat. She placed her head on top of it and nestled it until she was comfortable. Duke looked over at Willow's phone sitting on the seat and figured he could use it when he needed to make a call. This was turning out to be a bad idea, especially when he saw a highway patrol car riding four cars behind them.

"You better hope and pray that we make it to St. Louis safely, because I'm on the verge of doing something way out of my character." Duke grimaced.

****

JD and Yusuf sat in the parking lot anxiously waiting. JD has had one hell of a day, and it seemed like shit was starting to really work his nerves. He was put at ease when he sat and talked to Yanni about her leaving him without any warning. She explained that she was too far gone off drugs and that the only thing she felt was important were the drugs. JD understood because he dealt with dope fiends all the time. Some of his best soldiers and workers were on some type of dope, and their dependency on it helped him realize how much of a disease drug abuse was.

A silver Hyundai Elantra pulled unto the lot and came down the ramp. The driver pulled up a few parking spaces down from JD, but you couldn't see in his car because the windows were tinted. JD watched and observed someone sitting up in the back seat. He narrowed his eyes to make sure that this was the car that he was waiting on, and when the driver got out, he grabbed the handle and exited his vehicle.

JD had on a baseball cap pulled all the way down on his face. His hair was draped over his shoulders, and it hung to his waist. It was difficult to tell whether he was a girl or a boy, and that was the element of surprise he was going for. He continued to walk down the pathway toward the bathroom and stopped at the vending machine to pretend like he was about to get some snacks.

"You need to get out and use the bathroom because I'm not stopping until we get to St. Louis," said Duke, opening his door. He grabbed the keys out of the ignition and watched as a woman made her way toward the visitor's center. "You want something out of the vending machine?"

"Yeah," yawned Willow. "I am a bit hungry."

"Didn't nobody tell you to throw up all that shit you ate earlier." Duke chuckled.

"I'm fucking pregnant, and the ride made me hella nauseous," Willow frowned. "I'm glad you're getting a kick out of the shit." Duke got out, walked back to her door, and opened it. He put the child locks on the windows and doors after she threw his phone out of the window. "You got five minutes."

"Okay, boss," she replied. Willow grabbed her purse then headed toward the bathroom. A small smile spread across her face when she recognized the long hair and KC hat on the person standing at the vending machine. She continued to the bathroom and went inside to wait for JD to come get her. She gave a woman a hundred dollars to use her phone at the rest stop in Colorado. She called JD and told him that Duke had kidnapped her and that he was taking her back to St. Louis to give her to O'Bannon. She told him to track her phone and wait until they made it to Missouri before he made a move to get her. JD pulled up a map and told her to make sure they made a stop at the rest stop by Tipton, and he would be there to get her.

Duke stretched and adjusted his neck because he was stiff from doing all of the driving. He wanted to make Willow drive for a while, but he felt like her crazy ass might crash the car on purpose. He saw it was taking the woman a long time to get something out of the machine, so he decided to just go up to the visitor's center and grab the drinks first. He walked up the path and whistled a little tune to let the woman know that someone was coming up behind her. Duke stopped a few steps away from the machines and dug down into his pockets. JD turned around, lifted his baseball cap, and stared at Duke vehemently.

"You thought you was gone take my bitch and get away with it?" JD hissed. Duke looked up, and before he could react, JD reached back and punched Duke square in the nose. Duke fell back onto the concrete, and JD pulled out his knife. Duke was unconscious, and JD was a man on fire. He walked up on Duke and stood over him. Next, he checked his pockets and pulled out the car keys. JD took his wallet and money out of his pockets and stared down at Duke. Yusuf got out of the car and ran over to the women's restroom. He opened the door and went in to get Willow.

"Willow!" Yusuf shouted. "It's me, Yusuf. Come on. JD has knocked that clown out!" Willow came out of the stall and stared at Yusuf, uncertain. Yusuf held his hands out to the side and smiled. "You gone act like that, lil' ole black girl!" Willow smiled because Yusuf used to always say that to her when she was younger.

"Yusuf!" Willow called out and smiled. She ran up to him and hugged him tightly. "Let's go before someone else pulls up to this rest stop." They both exited the restroom to witness JD beating the shit out of Duke. JD had slapped Duke back to consciousness because he wanted Duke to be awake when he beat his ass. He punched Duke in the face repeatedly while he held the collar of his shirt.

Willow ran up and started kicking Duke in the side and punched him a few times in the face. She grabbed JD's knife off the ground and sliced Duke across the cheek with it. Duke screamed out in pain as blood sprayed on her shirt.

"I told you, bitch ass nigga, that I was gone get ya!" Willow taunted.

"Don't kill the nigga," JD instructed. "We just gon' leave his ass beat up at the rest stop. I was about to slit the nigga's throat, but I changed my mind. We gone catch up with his ass at another time, and maybe we can have that dude Locco take care of his ass."

"I'm sure he's going to be interested in hearing how this nigga jumped out on me at the hotel." Willow smiled. "Locco don't like yo' ass anyway, and I'm sure Shaggy's going to feel some type of way about the shit!"

"I… I was just trying to make a little cash," Duke cried. "I owe a lot on my mortgage, and my lazy ass wife doesn't want to work. I pay two leases on two Mercedes Coupes, and all three of my children attend private school, so I'm a little strapped for cash. Can't you understand why I was so desperate?"

"Don't nobody give a fuck about what you sayin'." JD frowned. "You were out of line, and you better be lucky I ain't killed your ass!"

"Come on, JD, and let's get the fuck out of here!" Yusuf yelled. "I'm sure the police will be making their rounds here soon, and I don't want to see them!"

"Okay, Unc, here we come," JD replied. He punched Duke a few more times, and Willow kicked him in the nuts for good measure.

"Bye, bitch ass nigga!" Willow yelled then laughed. She and JD ran over to the car and jumped in with the quickness. Duke was messed up pretty good, but that was the least of his worries because he had to get back to California somehow.

CHAPTER EIGHTEEN

"Why you so tense?" asked Indigo, walking up on Cypher. "I know exactly how to relax you if you let me." She wrapped her arms around Cypher's neck, and he pulled her off of him. She noticed that a loud smell of alcohol was seeping out of his pores, and she almost got drunk from smelling it.

"I ain't interested, Indigo," Cypher fussed. He frowned as he walked over toward the couch. "What the fuck do you want?"

"Is that any way to talk to the mother of your child?" she asked smugly.

"What the fuck did you just say?" Cypher snapped, not amused. Indigo smiled brightly at him because she was trying to get back into his good graces. No one was really fucking with her in the industry, and the only momentum that she got came from being tied to Cypher.

"I'm with child, and it's your baby," she announced proudly.

"The fuck it is!" Cypher shouted. "Your ass been sucking and fucking half of the music industry, and you think I'm going to fall for the okie doke?" Indigo's smile turned into a look of disgust as she stared at him, displeased by his response.

"For your information, stupid nigga, you were the only one I was fucking raw!" Indigo retorted. "I should have known your trifling ass was going to come out of a bag like this!" Truth be told, Indigo knew that Cypher wasn't the father, but she would try her best to convince him otherwise. "I don't know why you have such a problem with loving me, but I'm not going to let it upset me or the baby." Cypher glared at Indigo angrily because he couldn't believe that this bitch was trying to come at him with a pregnancy.

"Indigo, I know you're not pregnant, because, for the past few months, the only way my nut got inside of you is through your mouth," Cypher chuckled. "You can't get pregnant from sucking a lot of dick."

"Fuck you, Cypher!" she shouted. "For your information, I have a piece of paper to prove that I'm pregnant, and it's your baby!" Indigo reached into her Prada bag and pulled out a piece of paper. She handed it to Cypher and turned her lips up at him in satisfaction. He snatched the paper out of her hand and quickly opened it up. He scanned through it and saw that Indigo was 99.9 percent pregnant. There were several drunken nights when Cypher went over to her loft, and they had very indecent sex, so there was a possibility that he might be the daddy.

"Fuck! How did this shit happen?" Cypher yelled. "Willow is pregnant too, and she's—"

"She's not pregnant by you!" Indigo insisted. "She's pregnant by that black ass, fine nigga. What's his name? JD?" Cypher balled up the paper he was holding in anger.

"I don't give a fuck what his name is, bitch! Willow is supposed to be my bitch, and I'll be damned if another nigga is going to lay claim on my baby!" Cypher growled.

"You need to stop drinking because it's making you completely delusional," Indigo pointed out and laughed. "I heard what happened between the two of you, and it looks like she's not having it either. That's why she got the fuck out of your house." Cypher narrowed his eyes at Indigo because this bitch knew too much.

"Who the fuck you been talking to?" Cypher seethed.

"Don't worry about it," Indigo replied, rolling her eyes. "Just know that I know about what happened." Indigo flipped her hair over her shoulder and turned her lips up at him. "Do your nuts still hurt?"

"Big mouth bitch!" Cypher shouted before he grabbed her around the neck. "I'm so tired of you bumping your fucking gums about shit that doesn't concern your funky ass! You talk too much bitch, and maybe I need to teach your ass a lesson on keeping those dick beaters closed!" He lifted Indigo into the air as he squeezed his hand tighter around her throat. Her eyes watered as her feet kicked in the air, and she tried to pry his hands off her throat. "I could kill you right now, bitch, and hide your body in the basement!"

"Let her the fuck go!" shouted a familiar voice. Cypher turned around and saw three men standing before him dressed in all black with ski masks on and guns.

"What the fuck is this?" Cypher spat angrily. "Are they with you, bitch?" He looked at Indigo, and she was starting to turn colors from a lack of oxygen going to her brain.

"Let her the fuck go!" shouted the same man.

"I know that voice from somewhere," Cypher uttered. He had

drank a half of a gallon of vodka and wasn't feeling any pain. "I'm gone kill this bitch whether you like it or not!" The three men stared at Cypher, and the one man that was doing all the talking decided to do something. He pointed his gun at Cypher then turned and pointed it at a lamp. He fired a single shot into it, shattering the porcelain all over the table and floor.

"Let her the fuck go!" the man demanded. "Or the next bullet is going in your ass!" Cypher looked at him then dropped Indigo on the floor. She fell to her knees, trying to catch her breath. Cypher leaned over and spat smack dab in her face then looked up at the gunman smugly.

"Fuck this bitch!" Cypher mocked and laughed. "And fuck you too!" The largest of the three men walked over to Cypher and slapped him across the face with his gun. Cypher fell to the floor hard as blood dripped from his mouth.

"What your little punk ass is goin' to do is get up and go get all of your money and jewelry out of the safe," the man instructed. Cypher looked up at him and spat blood on the man's pants and shoes.

"Fuck you, fat boy!" Cypher shot back and let out a diabolical laugh. "All you niggas want to do is take my shit! I'm the one who's worked hard to get all of this, and you just want to come in and take it! Fuck all of you, including that nut rag bitch! She's probably in on this bullshit, and I promise that I will get all of you!" The gunman smacked Cypher with the butt of his gun and knocked him on conscious. He looked over at Indigo and got an idea.

"Do you know where he keeps all of his shit?" the man shouted.

Indigo had just gained her breath back, but she started hyperventilating when the large man approached her.

"No, sir," Indigo whimpered. "I just know that he keeps some stuff in his bedroom. Is his housekeeper here? Because she knows where he keeps everything." The man looked back at his counterparts then smacked Indigo in the face with his gun.

"Bitch, I think you're lying to me!" the man shouted.

"Hold the fuck up! That's not what we discussed!" stated the man who was doing the talking at first.

"Charisma!" Indigo blurted out. The other two men looked over at him then back at Indigo. "Charisma, why are you doing this?"

"Bitch, this ain't no Charisma," he replied, trying to disguise his voice. "Now, shut the fuck up!" He walked over to where she and the other masked man were standing, and he looked down at her. "Now, get the fuck up, and take us to the bedroom!" She noticed how intensely the man was looking at her. It was as if he were trying to warn her with his eyes.

Indigo opened the door to Cypher's master suite. She knew that Charisma was one of the gunmen, but she figured it would be best to just play along as if she'd made a mistake. She was very nervous because it seemed like the largest man didn't give a fuck about smacking her around. The side of her face ached from the blow he'd served her earlier. Indigo went over to the huge walk-in closet and opened the doors.

"This is where Cypher keeps all of his possessions. There are clothes worth thousands of dollars with price tags still on them. He keeps his watches and jewelry over there in that chest that's in the middle of the closet, and the last time I remembered, he has a safe in the wall behind his coats where he keeps his money. I don't know the combination, but I'm sure it might be open since Cypher was already home." Indigo moved to the side and watched as two of the men ran into the closet and started grabbing shit. The one gunman that Indigo suspected was Charisma just stood next to her and watched as the other men had their way in the closet.

"Hurry up, the both of you! If Cypher wakes up while we're in here, he might call the cops, and we're all fucked!" Charisma complained. The other two men ignored him and continued to load up the designer duffle bags that Cypher had in the closet.

"Why yo' bitch ass ain't grabbing shit?" asked one of the men.

"Because I don't want none of this shit! Don't worry about me. Just hurry the fuck up!" Charisma leaned down and whispered into Indigo's ear. "You're going to be okay. Just do what I tell you, and things will go smoothly." Indigo looked up at him wearily and shook her head.

"You got me fucked up! I'm gone show you niggas!" Cypher shouted vehemently. He raised his gun and started firing shots randomly toward the closet. Charisma hit the floor, and before he could pull Indigo to the floor, two shots hit her in the chest, and she collapsed. Charisma looked at her blood-stained body with a mortified look on his face. Cypher continued shooting as he approached the opening of the closet. His gun ran out of bullets, and he pulled another one out of his waistband. He pulled back the hammer and started firing again recklessly toward the men.

"Fuck you, Cypher!" shouted one of the other men, and he started firing shots back at Cypher. It didn't do much good, because as soon as he jumped out into the open, he was hit several times by Cypher.

Cypher looked down at Indigo and noticed one of the gunmen lying next to her. He saw how the gunman was reacting to Indigo and was about to fire a shot into his head when he heard a loud bang and felt a burning sensation in the shoulder of the arm that he was using to hold his gun. Cypher yelled out in pain, and his arm dropped to his side as the large gunman charged toward him. Cypher raised his gun, but the man on the floor grabbed Cypher's ankle, causing him to tumble down to the floor. The large man ran up to Cypher and hit him in the head with his gun, knocking Cypher unconscious again.

"Let's get the fuck out of here!" the large man shouted.

"What about Jay?" Charisma called out.

"Fuck that nigga! He's dead!" The large man uttered before he kicked Cypher in the side. Charisma stared down at Indigo's lifeless body, feeling distraught and pained. He was in love with Indigo, and it was his child that she was carrying.

CHAPTER NINETEEN

*Y*usuf pulled up in front of the house with JD following him in the Elantra. JD was so grateful that Willow was unharmed that he continuously thanked Allah for this blessing. They didn't get to talk much, because she was too tired to even keep her eyes open, and it didn't help that the sky was pitch black either. She managed to kiss all over JD's face and nestled up against his arm while they rode the rest of the way to the farm.

"Willow, wake up, baby," JD cooed, shaking her lightly. He moved the hair out of her face then kissed her lips softly because he was so relieved to have her with him. Willow's eyes shot open, and she felt discombobulated, so she swung wildly at JD, hitting him in the eye. "Damn, girl! What the fuck you on?" JD shouted. Willow stopped with a confused look on her face as she stared at JD for a second. "You're safe Lil' Baby," he assured her, and that's when Willow remembered that she was rescued by her lover.

"I'm sorry, baby," Willow uttered, grabbing JD's face. She kissed his lips softly, and a pleasant smile appeared across hers. "Thank you, Big Baby, for coming to get me. You saved my life, my king!" She took his baseball cap off and placed it backward on her head.

"You know I wasn't gone leave my queen in the hands of some sucka muthafucka!" JD shot back. "I love you, Lil' Baby, and I'm sorry that I put you in harm's way. I'm so glad to have you here safely with me, and I'm not letting you out of my sight ever again!"

"You promise?" Willow asked, taking two handfuls of his hair.

"I put that on my life!" JD replied then he kissed her passionately on the lips. "C'mon, so I can put you in a bath." A big smile spread across Willow's lips.

"Is that all you're going to do?" she asked seductively.

"I'm gone dig all in them guts Lil' Baby, don't worry," JD assured her. "I just got to clean that puss first, and get it to the flavor that I like."

"And what's that?" Willow questioned curiously. JD looked at her with a smirk on his face.

"Cocoa butter and black cherry with a hint of sugar and spice," he replied lustfully. "My most favorite things!"

Willow was soaking in an old-fashioned, clawfoot tub filled with hot water, cocoa butter oil, and bubbles. JD had drawn her a bath before he went downstairs to make the love of his life something to eat. Willow was hot and horny once JD laid that steamy kiss on her in the car. She was damn near on his lap when he stopped her and told her she needed to get in the tub and eat something before he tore that pussy up. Willow wanted to protest his decision at first but changed her mind after she realized that she did need to freshen up before making love to her fiancé. The shower she'd taken at the seedy hotel didn't make her feel clean. Also, she'd peed so many damn times that she didn't want JD putting his lips on her pissy pussy. The bath was feeling wonderful, and what came after it was going to be epic!

"I know your greedy ass is ready to eat," JD joked. walking into the bathroom.

"You bet yo' sweet ass I am!" she called out, laughing. "What you got for me?"

"I made you a turkey burger with lettuce, tomato, cheese, pickles, mayo, and mustard. Also, I cut you some french fries out of a few potatoes 'cause I know that's how you like your fries," JD mentioned sincerely. Willow's face lit up, and a big smile spread across her face. JD did know her like the back of his hand, and that was the one thing Willow loved most about him.

"You take such good care of me," Willow gushed. "And you'll be proud of me. I ate a lot of fresh vegetables while I was in California! Everything seemed to be organic."

"That's good, Lil' Baby," he replied. JD sat the tray down on a stool sitting next to the tub. He kissed Willow on the forehead then walked toward the door.

"Where are you going? Ain't you gone sit in here with me?" Willow whined.

"I need to put some sheets on the bed and get the room ready for you. There's a robe hanging on the back of the door that you can use when you get out of the tub. I just want you to eat and relax, Willow. I'm not going anywhere. I'll be waiting for you when you get out. Okay?" She stuck her bottom lip out at him and pouted.

"Okay," she whined as JD walked out of the bathroom. Willow looked over at the burger then picked it up off the plate. Her stomach was in her back, and she was ready to smash her food. She opened her mouth and took a bite of the sandwich. She closed her eyes and chewed with great satisfaction because she managed to get the perfect bite with just enough meat and all the fixings. This was going to be a swift love affair, and the end result will be Willow devouring her burger in four seconds flat.

Willow walked into the room, and it was decorated with candles and wildflowers. The cozy feeling that the eclectic farmhouse gave Willow made her feel like she was a part of a romantic movie with a starring role. It was apparent that JD had taken his time and decorated the room with nothing but love. Tears welled up in Willow's eyes because she realized that JD had set up a romantic setting for her, and it melted her heart. She walked over to the bed, taking in all the beautiful aspects of the room. She climbed up on it to wait for her beloved. She wasn't quite sure where JD had gone, but she knew he would be in there soon enough.

JD had decided to jump in the shower after Willow got out of the tub. He set the room up with candles and flowers for her and figured she'd be a little full and tired after devouring her dinner. He had gone downstairs to wash the dishes he'd left after making her food, and he laughed at the empty plate when he entered the bathroom. After his shower, he wrapped up in a towel and entered into the bedroom. JD was ready to kiss his sweetie all over her body because he missed the soft feel of her skin and the sweet smell of cocoa butter when he held her in his arms. His dick was rock hard from the anticipation of making love to her, but when he looked over at Willow, she was fast asleep.

JD walked over to the bed and smiled as he stared at Willow. He climbed up on the mattress and nestled up behind her. He opened her robe and rubbed his hand across her belly. The thought of the stress that Willow had been under these past few days made JD worry. He knew that a miscarriage could potentially happen according to the articles he had been reading on Google, and that was the last thing that he wanted to occur. Willow began to stir as JD's hand moved down to her pelvis, and he slid his fingers in between her legs. He rubbed them against her clit and kissed her neck softly before he pushed them inside of her folds. Willow moaned as JD continued to pleasure her, and she reached her arm behind her to grab the back of his neck.

"I've missed your touch," she whined, spreading her legs further apart. "Make love to me, JD, please!"

"In due time, Lil' Baby." JD chuckled. "I just want to take my time and bask in the softness of your body." He grazed his fingers over Willow's nipple then pinched and pulled at it, making her moan with pleasure. His firm erection pressed against her ass, and she could feel his stiffness through the fabric of her robe. All of her senses were heightened by the sensory overload that JD was providing, and she didn't know how much longer she could last before she exploded with all the feeling and touching.

Willow pulled away from JD and slid out of her robe. His towel was already undone, and his erection was sticking up like it was happy to see her. Willow looked at JD seductively then grabbed a hold of his rod. She smiled at him devilishly before she went to work with a little teasing of her own. She licked around the head of his dick then slid it into her mouth.

"Oh shit!" JD called out as she deep throated him a few times. She took all of his length down her throat and let it linger for a second before she came back up off of it. She stared deeply into his eyes while she stroked his shaft. JD sat up and kissed her lips quickly in approval then Willow went back down on him hungrily. She slobbered and bobbed on his hard dick while JD stroked her hair and moaned. He reached one of his hands down and pinched her nipple as she continued to give him some of the best head yet. She could tell that he was moments away from having a full orgasm, so she slowly slid her tongue up his shaft and made a smacking noise when she popped the head out of her mouth.

"That shit felt so good, Willow. Come here!" JD grabbed Willow and kissed her passionately as he pulled her on his lap. Willow reached down in between her legs and inserted JD's rock-hard dick inside of her.

"Aaaahhhhh," she gasped, holding her head back. JD reached up and took both of her breasts in his hands and started pinching her nipples while she rocked back and forth on top of him. He put one of them inside of his mouth and bit down as she wrapped her arms around his neck. "Shit, you feel so good inside me. I craved this big muthafucka while I was away from you," she uttered. "Don't you ever leave me alone again!" JD could hear her voice trembling, and when he felt his shoulder getting wet, his emotions suddenly overtook him.

JD wrapped his arms around Willow's waist and hugged her tightly. He tried to stop her body's motion as she continued to rock against him, but Willow continued to fuck. He wanted to pull her away so that he could wipe her tears, but she nestled her face into his neck and held on to her arms tightly, not wanting to let go.

"Willow, baby, please look at me," JD begged.

"No," she whimpered, continuing to rock on him.

"I need to see your face, Lil' Baby," he demanded. "Please, don't do this to me!" He could hear her sniffling as his shoulder continued to get wetter, and his heart was aching as she cried. All of the emotions that both of them were feeling had become too much for him to bear, so JD flipped over, placing Willow on her back. "I know I fucked up, Lil' Baby, and if I could do it all over again, I would do things differently. Please look at me, Willow! Please!" JD pleaded. Willow slowly pulled away from JD, and he could see all the hurt and sorrow on her face. He urgently wiped all the tears from her face and kissed her lips several times in the process.

"JD, it's okay," Willow sobbed. "I'm just happy to be here in your arms again, and it feels so good being loved by you; that's all, baby."

"I'm happy that you're here too, and we're going to get married as soon as we get back to St Louis," JD assured her. "I've talked to Keena, and she's working on shit for us." Willow looked at him in surprise and smiled.

"You're trusting Keena to handle our wedding plans?" Willow replied, intrigued.

"Well, Granny is helping her as well, and she reached out to a friend of hers to help," JD explained. "I know it's our big day, and you might have wanted to be involved, but you mean so much to me that I wanted to do it as a surprise."

"None of it really matters to me," Willow confessed. "Just as long as I'm married to you. That's the only thing that matters to me!" She smiled warmly as JD leaned down and kissed her lips. She slithered her tongue inside of his mouth, and his dick instantly became hard again. Willow pulled away from JD and stared at him for a second, lovingly. "Can we finish?"

"Damn straight!" JD uttered. He reached down and rubbed his erection against her soft, wet folds then plunged his thickness inside of her. Willow closed her eyes and sighed happily as JD made love to her until they both collapsed from being exhausted. They fell fast asleep in each other's arms and had the best sleep because of it.

CHAPTER TWENTY

The Next Day

Keena was hard at work filling out the invitations for JD and Willow's reception. He had put her and Granny on the task of getting things together because he wanted to marry Willow as soon as possible. Keena took her job seriously and wanted to make their reception epic. JD wanted to have a small intimate wedding ceremony with just the family for the nuptials then have a huge block party in front of his granny's house with a two-block radius cut off to traffic. Granny made the necessary phone call to the alderman and got all of the needed permits to make this happen. She was so excited about the two of them getting married and took on the full responsibility of catering the food for the affair. They ordered tents, tables, and chairs to set out in the middle of the street for people to sit at. Also, they got a DJ and portable dance floor to place on one of the vacant lots so that everyone would have somewhere to party. No one had ever done anything like this, and considering JD and Willow were the king and queen of their hood, this type of celebration was absolutely fitting for them.

"Did you remember to fill out an invitation for Melody?" Granny asked, sticking a stamp on an invitation.

"Yes, ma'am," Keena replied. "I knew she would pitch a fit if we didn't send her one. I wonder if there's a way we can have her call to listen to the ceremony?"

"She usually calls me every couple of days, so if she calls me beforehand, I can tell her what time the ceremony is taking place," Granny explained. "I'm so excited about this wedding, and I'm surprised that Willow went along with everything since it's such short notice."

"I talked to her this morning, and she said she's absolutely fine with us handling everything," Keena explained. "She said that JD wanted to be in charge of all of it to keep her from stressing out since she's carrying his baby. The only thing she asked is that we have white roses and lilies for the flowers and all of the guests wear white to the reception."

"That sounds easy enough," Granny replied. "But if my memory serves me correctly, JD said that he and his boys are wearing some orange and blue as well."

"I remembered that too," Keena replied. "JD wants us to wear either orange or blue Chuck Taylor tennis shoes, and we're all supposed to go shopping when he and Willow touch down."

"I'm sure they both will be too tired to do anything when they get here," Granny laughed. "That drive is a bit tiresome, and I know Willow is definitely not going to be in the mood to do anything but eat and sleep! She drove all the way from California to Missouri, and that's not an easy drive." JD or Willow bothered to tell either of them about the circumstances surrounding Willow's trip back home. They felt the least they knew the better.

"I'm sure," Keena laughed heartily. She knew that pregnancy tended to make the average woman lazy, and JD didn't let Willow do much of anything once he found out that she was with child.

Keena and Granny continued to talk and work on stuff for the wedding. They were so excited about it, and couldn't wait until the couple made it home so they could show them what they've already accomplished. Granny saw a shadowy figure walk across her porch to the door, and she wondered who it could be.

"Let me see who this is about to knock on my door," said Granny, getting up out of her chair. She wasn't expecting anyone, and people don't generally knock on her door. There was stuff all over the living room floor, and she really didn't want anyone coming inside to disrupt all of their hard work. Granny went over to the door and slowly opened it up. A sarcastic smirk appeared across her face when she saw her grandbaby standing in front of her. "What you doing here, Patsy?"

"Why do you always act like it's a problem when I come see you, Granny?" asked Patsy defensively. "Maybe I just wanted to see my grandmother."

"Riiiight," said Granny, unlatching the screen door. "Come on in and watch your walking. I don't want you to step on any of these invitations or fuck something up!"

"Why do you have invitations all over the place?" Patsy asked, stepping into the house. She looked around, staring at all the invitations and other decorations scattered all over the room. She wondered what was going on and would she be invited to participate in whatever was about to happen.

"We're getting stuff ready for JD and Willow's wedding," Granny explained with excitement in her voice.

"I know you said they were getting married, but how soon is this taking place?" Patsy blurted out in shock. Keena glared over at Patsy with a frown on her face then looked at Granny. She knew who Patsy was, and figured she would be relieved now that she didn't have to worry about Willow fucking with O'Bannon.

"Are you sure we should tell her anything?" Keena questioned. "I'm sure she's going to break her neck to go tell O'Bannon and throw it up in his face." Patsy looked over at Keena feeling a bit defensive.

"Excuse me," Patsy scoffed. "Who the hell are you?"

"I'm Willow's best friend if you must know," Keena shot back. "And I damn sure know who you are!"

"Granny, you better get this girl," Patsy seethed arrogantly. She looked Keena up and down before she rolled her eyes hard.

"I ain't got to do shit!" Granny scoffed. "And Keena's probably right now that I think about it."

"What!" Patsy shouted in outrage. "I can't believe you're siding with her, Granny!"

"Please believe it, dear," Granny replied. "As a matter of fact, what brings you over, Patsy? Are you trying to see if JD and Willow have returned from out of town?" Patsy looked at her grandmother funny because that was exactly why she was over there. O'Bannon had told her that Duke would be arriving with Willow sometime today, but he hadn't heard from Duke, so he was worried that something had happened.

"I told you, Granny. I came to see you," Patsy replied. "I don't know why y'all think that O'Bannon controls my every move."

"Don't he?" Keena asked sarcastically. "I know he used to control Willow to a certain extent, so I have no doubt he has your ass hoppin', skippin', and jumpin' at his every command." Granny chuckled, but Patsy didn't find it funny.

"For your information, I call my own shots," Patsy snapped. "You see O'Bannon stopped coming around and being with Willow."

"But he's made up for it these past few weeks, trying to beg my homegirl to take his raggedy ass back!" Keena retorted.

"Ain't shit raggedy about my husband, honey, so get your facts straight!" Patsy snapped. "He's got more class than JD, and he's definitely dipping in the slums by fucking with Willow! I never understand the appeal myself, because she's just another ghetto hoodrat like all the rest of you!" Keena put her pen down and jumped up from the couch.

"Excuse my language, Granny, but this ugly, black bitch got me totally fucked up! You ain't about to sit here and disrespect my friend like that while she's not here to defend herself, 'cause we both know that if she were here, she would punch you in yo' mouth with the quickness!" Keena snapped. "And if you keep talking shit, I'm gone be the one to punch you in yo' shit!"

"Whatever," Patsy scoffed, waving her hand in a dismissive manner. Keena walked around the coffee table and headed toward Patsy when Granny stopped her.

"Keena, baby," said Granny sweetly. "Can I have you run to the store and get me some cigarettes?" Keena stopped in her tracks and looked at Granny. Next, she glared over at Patsy and narrowed her eyes.

"Yeah, I'll go get you some cigarettes," she replied hesitantly. She really wanted to beat Patsy's ass, but she didn't want to disrespect Granny's house. "Is there anything else you want?"

"That's it, baby," Granny replied. She reached in her bra and pulled out a few bills to give to Keena.

"It's all good, Granny," said Keena, making her way over to the door. "They're on me today." Granny walked over to the door with Keena to make sure that she didn't try to reach out and hit Patsy. Keena left, but Patsy still wasn't safe just yet. She had pissed Granny off with her words, and one thing about Granny, she was going to let Patsy know how she felt whether it hurt her feelings or not.

"You're not happy unless someone's going off on you," Granny spat in disgust. "Don't be talking bad about Willow, because yo' pedophile ass man couldn't keep his hands off of her!"

"Granny..."

"Don't *Granny* me! I don't want to hear the shit, and I'm gone ask yo' ass again... Why are you here, Patsy?"

"Because I have a problem, and I felt like you was the only person I could talk to about the situation," Patsy replied nervously. She realized that she had pissed her grandmother off and memories of ass whooping's past came flooding her psyche.

"So, what's up?" Granny snapped. Patsy looked at her with a confused look on her face then she walked over and sat down on the couch. Her palms were sweaty, and she fidgeted with her shirt anxiously.

"Well, Granny, you know that my husband is in the hospital because he was hit by a car, and you know O'Bannon's pretty upset with Willow because she decided to be with JD and not him," Patsy rambled.

"Get on with it, girl, and cut to the chase. Keena will be back in a minute," Granny complained. A slight frown came across Patsy's face because Granny was being curt with her, and she didn't like it.

"Anyway... O'Bannon knows who hit him with the car, and he wants me to lie to the police and tell them that JD was the one who did it," Patsy blurted out uncomfortably.

"Did you see who done it?" Granny asked frankly.

"No, ma'am," Patsy uttered.

"So, that means you tell that muthafucka that you ain't lying to police for him! Don't you know your stupid ass can go to jail for that shit? That's called falsifying information, dummy! Is O'Bannon's raggedy ass worth your freedom?"

"Uh... no, ma'am," Pasty uttered. "But he's my husband, and O'Bannon is going to be very upset with me if I don't do it."

"I guess you're stuck between a rock and a hard place because worrying about O'Bannon being mad is going to be the least of your worries," Granny assured Patsy. "'Cause if JD gets locked up behind this shit, then Willow's going to fuck the both of you up, and that's something that you're not ready for!" Patsy looked at her grandmother with a worried expression on her face. She knew that JD could be a muthafucka in his own right, but she had no idea what Willow might do.

CHAPTER TWENTY-ONE

"*It* feels good to be home." Willow sighed as the familiar sights of the neighborhood moved past her eyes.

"It does," JD agreed. "But we have a lot to do before Saturday when you become my wife!" He was about to pull up in front of the apartment, but Willow stopped him before he made the turn at the corner.

"Hey! Park in the back of the house," Willow instructed.

"For what?" JD scoffed. "You know I don't like going up them back steps, Lil' Baby." Willow lifted an eyebrow at him and turned up her lips.

"Boy, look! Just do what I asked you to do," she scoffed. "It must be a good reason if I asked you to do it."

"All right, woman," JD replied a bit annoyed. He turned into the alley and pulled up to their backyard. "Get yo' ass out and unlock the gate since you wanted us to pull up in the back."

"Gladly." Willow smiled. "And when you see why I wanted you to do this, your ass will certainly owe me an apology."

"Not if you're keeping secrets," JD replied. "We're about to be married, so you can't be keeping shit from me."

"Maybe the only thing I was focused on was being in your arms, Big Baby, when I saw you," Willow offered. JD's brow furrowed.

"You know I hate when you call me that," JD complained.

"And it's obvious I don't give a fuck," Willow replied and hopped out the car quickly. JD chuckled because he tried to grab her, but she was too fast for him.

"You gotta be quicker than that!" Willow laughed. She took her key and unlocked the deadbolt lock that was on the chain that held the fence together. Next, she unwrapped it and pulled the gate open so that JD could pull the car into the yard. "I'm going to go unlock the door while you pull in. It would be best if you backed into the yard," she suggested. JD looked at her crazy then did what she asked.

Willow walked up to the back door and opened it with the key. Next, she walked back downstairs and went to the back of the car. JD popped the trunk and got out the car because he was interested in why she was going through all of this trouble.

"I'm tellin' you, nigga, you gon' have to bow down to a bitch after this one," Willow gloated. She grabbed the bottom of the trunk and lifted it.

"I don't see shit but all of your stuff." JD chuckled. Willow turned her lips up at him and smirked.

"Wait for it, nigga," she replied arrogantly. She grabbed the lining on the side of the trunk and pulled it back. JD's mouth fell open when he saw bricks of cocaine lined throughout the interior. They were stacked on top of each other, and it looked like there were at least twelve on the one side.

"What the fuck, Lil' Baby!" JD shouted. He grabbed Willow and kissed her lips passionately because she'd just made a major score. His hands slid down to her ass, and he gripped it firmly. Willow giggled and wrapped her arms around his neck while they tongue kissed nastily in celebration.

"Wait a minute, JD." Willow giggled, pulling away from him. "Let's get this shit into the house then we can finish what we started. Can you go and get a couple of trash bags out of your kitchen?"

"You right for telling me to go get them out of my kitchen." JD laughed, smacking Willow on the butt. He walked up the steps and went into the house while Willow laughed at her man.

JD and Willow took all of the dope out of the car and decided to leave it parked in the backyard until Willow called Locco to see what to do with it. She was so happy to be back in JD's arms that she didn't mentioned what happened in California. She finally explained to JD how she came to acquire the blessing, and even though JD was pissed off that her life was put in danger by some random nigga, he was proud that his Lil' Baby had enough sense to get herself out of the jam.

JD walked into Willow's apartment and watched as she danced around the kitchen. The music was pumping through her stereo, and he liked the way her ass was shaking in the little bitty shorts she was wearing. He made his way behind her and placed his hands on her hips. He pumped his stiffness against her ass, and a big smile spread across her face when she looked back at him.

"You came to bow down, huh, nigga?" Willow gloated. JD hid the dope in the floor where he generally kept his supply. He had to move the couch and area rug, but it was well worth it at the beginning and end of the day.

"I ain't bowing down to shit, but I'll give you your props, Lil' Baby." JD smiled. He turned her around and kissed her lips firmly. He grabbed the bottom of her t-shirt and pulled it over her head. A wicked smile appeared on her face and she gasped when he clamped down on her nipple.

"Emmmm," she moaned. "Get down on your knees, and do that thing I like!"

"I don't know what you're talking about," mumbled JD as he continued to suck her nipple.

"Yeah... play dumb if you want to," Willow replied. She pushed JD off of her and covered her breasts with both hands. "I guess I'm just going to go back to what I was doing." She went to pick up her shirt, and JD swept her up off her feet.

"No, yo' ass ain't!" JD called out and laughed. He smacked Willow on the ass and took her into the bedroom. He threw her down on the bed, and she bounced on top of it like a rag doll. Willow tried to move across the bed quickly to get away, but JD grabbed her by the ankles. "Get yo' ass back here!" He pulled her to him and unfastened his pants. He licked his lips while she watched him seductively because she knew he was about to do what she wanted. "Spread 'em!"

"Nope!" Willow protested. She cut his eyes at him and slowly laid on her back. She placed her hand in between her legs and started to play with her pussy. JD bit down on his bottom lip and enjoyed the show Willow was putting on for him. He took his hands and placed them on her knees then opened her legs wider so he could see her welcoming folds. "In nine months, your child will be coming out of there." Willow giggled.

"I know," he replied happily. "And I can't wait to meet him or her." JD leaned down and kissed Willow's lips. Next, he moved down to her neck and nibbled on it for a second. He trailed his tongue further down until he landed at her well-trimmed bush. "Open it up for me," JD ordered. Willow reached down and opened her wet walls. "Stick your fingers inside and give me a taste." She did as she was told and plunged her fingers inside of her wetness. She slowly pulled them out and placed them against JD's lips. He opened his mouth, and Willow slid them inside with a big grin on her face. "Delicious!"

"Emmm hmmm." Willow giggled then gasped as JD licked up her pussy lips. "Ohhh!" she uttered quickly because JD stuck his tongue between her folds, and when he latched onto her clit, she almost climaxed instantly. "My God!"

"Mmmmm," JD moaned against it and Willow screamed out in ecstasy.

"I'm about to cum. Aaaaaaaaaa!" Willow called out, but JD didn't let up. He reached his hands up and started pinching and pulling her nipples. Willow arched her back and continued to moan from all of the stimulation her Big Baby was providing for her. Willow looked down between her legs, and all she saw was hair. She let out a little laugh, but it was soon interrupted by the second orgasm that was about to hit her. "Uuuuuuuuuuhhhhhhhhhh!" grunted Willow as her body shook like never before. JD still wasn't letting up, and he continued to satisfy all of her body with both his hands and mouth. "I love you, Julio Delgado!" Willow proclaimed as tears welled up in her eyes. She became overwhelmed with emotion, and the tears just flowed as a third orgasm hit her. "Fuuuuuuuck!"

JD came up off her and stood to his feet. He moved his hair out of his face and saw his lover crying. He climbed in between her legs and leaned over her with love in his eyes.

"Ain't nothing wrong, JD," Willow confessed. "I'm just emotional."

"I know, Lil' Baby," JD replied with a slight smile on his face. He leaned down and kissed her lips softly. Willow slipped her tongue inside of his mouth, and they kissed passionately for a few minutes. Willow felt some pressure between her legs and opened her eyes wide when she realized that JD had pushed his dick inside of her wet, aching walls. His girth filled her, and she pushed her pelvis up to meet JD's strokes. Their kiss turned nasty as he continued to go deeper and deeper inside of Willow. She wrapped her arms around his neck and continued to meet his stroke each time he pushed down. They were doing their own dance while "Beauty" by Dru Hill soared through the air.

"Wait a minute! Wait a minute!" Willow breathed breathlessly.

"Are you okay, Lil' Baby?" JD panicked.

"I'm fine, baby," she giggled. "I want some doggy style that's all." A smirk appeared on JD's face as his eyes gleamed.

"Me too!" JD replied enthusiastically. "Turn over!" He pulled out and watched as Willow lifted up and turned over on her stomach. She lifted her hips up off the bed and placed her knees down into the mattress. JD slapped her ass and licked up the creases of her pussy before he slid himself inside of her slowly. He pulled her by the hips to the edge of the bed, and she pressed the back of her feet against the side of it. JD pulled back then pushed all of him deep inside of Willow. She moaned and wiggled her ass because she wanted to make sure all of him was inside. He eased back a little then served her with several long, deep strokes before he gripped her thighs and started jamming his stiffness inside of her. Willow called out in pleasurable pain while she played with her clit. His big dick felt so good going inside her tight walls, but all she wanted was for JD to nut. She knew if they did it doggy style, he'd cum a lot quicker. However, she found herself orgasm before him, and she didn't care, because it felt like her entire body was tingling when it hit. Willow had a euphoric feeling that took over her being as she screamed out one last time. Her body slumped down, and she fell to the bed, but JD didn't let up. He laid down on her back and humped a few more times before he let out his own howl. He dug a little deeper as he released his seed inside of her. JD was exhausted, and he kissed her shoulder blade before he laid his face against her damp skin.

"Lil' Baby, I don't approve of what you did in California, but I can respect you for it," JD admitted. "And because of your actions, we gone be set for sure, and I promise that we gon' be done with this shit once all of this dope is gone." He slid himself out of Willow and pulled her on top of him. She turned over and intertwined her legs between JD's. Next, she wrapped her arm around his waist and grabbed his hand.

"Whatever you say," Willow replied. "You're the leader of our household, but I hope you're going to be respectful and open to my opinions."

"No doubt," JD agreed. "We in this shit together… until death do us part." He leaned over and kissed Willow's lips.

"Until death do us part," she replied. Willow nestled against JD and took in the scent of his essence. "Big Baby?"

"What, Lil' Baby?"

"I'm hungry. Can you fix me something to eat?" Willow asked and giggled.

"Yo' ass always hungry." JD chuckled. "But it's whatever my queen desires."

CHAPTER TWENTY-TWO

"*W*here the fuck are you, and why haven't I heard from your ass?" O'Bannon snapped angrily. "You should have been in St. Louis since yesterday!"

"You wouldn't believe what happened to me," Duke replied. "I don't have Willow, and it's all bad."

"What the fuck do you mean?" O'Bannon shouted. "I thought you said you had her secure in the back seat of the car! Did you let her get away, or did she get to you and you released her?" Duke held the phone out from his ear. He was in a lot of pain from the four broken ribs JD had given him. Also, the doctor said he was severely dehydrated by the time some random strangers found him behind the visitor's center where JD had left him.

"Shut the fuck up for a second and listen!" Duke shouted. "I'm done with this stupid shit! You couldn't pay me enough money to continue on this ridiculous path you have me on! I almost lost my life trying to help you out! Somehow, Willow was able to get in touch with that lil' nigga she fucks with, and he ambushed me at the rest stop. I have four broken ribs, and I almost died from dehydration. If you want that bitch so bad, you go get her yourself!" Duke hung up the phone and threw it on the side of the bed. He was finished doing O'Bannon's dirty work when it came to that little bitch, Willow. She was more trouble than what she's worth, and Duke had his fill of the bullshit. He tried to call Shaggy, but for some reason, his calls kept going to voicemail. He thought Willow might have called and tipped Shaggy off about what he'd done, and that wouldn't be a good thing if Locco found out!

O'Bannon was lying in bed fuming when Patsy walked into the room. She had a worried look on her face, but as usual, it was not a concern of O'Bannon's. His plan to get Willow back had gone to shit, and he knew the probability of Willow trying to get at him was going to be a definite.

"Where the fuck have you been?" O'Bannon grumbled. "I haven't seen your ass since yesterday morning." Patsy looked at O'Bannon and rolled her eyes.

"One of us has to keep our business afloat. We have an event coming up in a few days, and I had a lot to do in order to make sure it goes well," Patsy explained. "What bug has flown up your ass?" O'Bannon glared at her.

"Did you get in touch with the detective yet?"

"No," Patsy replied. "And I don't think I'm going to either." O'Bannon's eyes widened because he couldn't believe what he was hearing.

"What the fuck did you just say to me?" he snapped. "Bitch! If I tell your black ass to do something, then, bitch, you better do it!"

"You know what, O'Bannon? Fuck you!" Patsy shouted. "All I've ever done was try to appease and satisfy your raggedy ass only for you to continuously make an ass out of me, and I'm fucking sick of it! I won't be making any report, and FYI..." Patsy walked over to the door. "Willow is marrying JD tomorrow, and there's nothing your ass can do about it! She's going to have JD's baby, and for some strange reason, I'm happy for them, so do with that what you want, bitch ass nigga! Oh... and I will be filing for divorce from your stupid ass based on the terms of our prenuptial agreement."

"Bitch, I'll kill you first!" O'Bannon howled. Patsy looked at him and smiled before she walked out of the hospital room. "Patsy! Get the fuck back here! Ricky! Ricky, where the fuck are you!" Ricky was down the hall with Patsy by the time O'Bannon started screaming both of their names. He decided to leave with his lover because Ricky knew that Patsy was the one with all the real money, and his bread would be buttered better with her knife.

****

"I can't believe you and JD are getting married tomorrow," Keena gushed. "If someone would have told me that a few years ago, I probably would have laughed in their face."

"I know, right?" Willow agreed. "I never in a million years thought that I would be marrying JD. However, they say sometimes the one that's directly in your face is the one that truly loves you."

"And I think that's the truth in your case," Keena replied. "What happened up in Cali that you weren't answering your phone? JD was going nuts not talking to you, and he called my ass a million times!"

"Nothing but a lot of bullshit," Willow replied. She walked over and sat on the couch next to Keena. They were chilling in Keena's apartment while they waited for JD to go to the mall. "Cypher got extra pissed at me because I told him the truth about my baby. He had the nerve to think that it's his!" Willow laughed hysterically, but Keena just sat there looking at her uncomfortably. "Why you ain't laughing? I figured you'd find the humor in the entire situation."

"Willow, there's something I need to tell you, and I probably should have told you when it first happened," Keena replied uncomfortably. Willow looked at her curiously because she wasn't sure what Keena was about to say to her.

"You're not about to confess some shit that you've done behind my back?" Willow asked anxiously. "You haven't fucked JD, have you? 'Cause if that's the case then I'm gone skin both you muthafuckas alive!"

"Calm down, Willow! I didn't fuck JD, but if I have to confess some shit, then I sucked his dick when we were twelve in Granny's backyard. He dared me to do it and said that he would give me five dollars." Willow looked at her in disbelief.

"Do you think I give a fuck about you sucking JD's dick when you were twelve? He used to dare me to do it too, but I wasn't into no shit like that, 'cause I was too young," Willow explained. "My brother said he would beat my ass if he found out I was having sex. I was supposed to wait until I got married, but we see that epically failed." Both women laughed for a second.

"Somebody should have told O'Bannon that shit," Keena said sarcastically.

"Bitch! You didn't fuck O'Bannon, did you?" Willow called out accusingly.

"Hell to the naw!" Keena shouted. "That's all you, boo! That's all you! He's fine and all, but I don't do stalkers. It's too much work trying to elude them." Willow narrowed her eyes at her friend because some of the shit that came out of her mouth amazed her. "Look, Willow, stop trying to figure it out. I'm just going to tell you and then we can talk about it."

"Fine, bitch! You ain't got to get all jumpy," Willow shot back. Keena looked at Willow and shook her head. She took a deep breath because she knew that Willow was about to have a conniption. "State yo' peace, heffa! Why you taking so long?"

"Cypher raped me at the music festival, and it happened right before you saved his life," Keena spat out quickly. She literally vomited the words out of her mouth, and they stumped Willow for a second.

"Huh?" Willow uttered.

"I know I should have told you when it happened, but so much was going on, and I was in shock. I didn't tell JD about it until last week when he was looking for you. I didn't know that you went to California, and when he told me, I freaked out and told him the truth!" Willow was stunned and at a loss for words.

"I saved that bitch ass nigga's life!" Willow shouted angrily. "If I would have known that he did that shit to you, I would have shot that muthafucka myself! How could you keep something like this from me? We're supposed to be best friends… sisters!"

"I know, Willow, but I just didn't want to mess things up between you and Cypher. Besides, you know people tend to slander the victim 'cause Cypher is famous." Willow jumped up from her seat.

"So what you saying, bitch, is that you thought I would be on that bitch ass niggas side?" Willow shouted angrily. "We've been through too much together for me to ever side with an off-brand muthafucka! Bitch, it's me and you forever, so you know I would always ride with you!"

"I'm sorry, Willow!" Keena sobbed. "I fucked up, and I really don't have anything else to say about it. Charisma came and found me in his tent, crying and distraught. He felt so bad about what happened to me, and he promised that Cypher would pay for his actions."

"We could have handled it right then and there!" Willow snapped. "I can't believe you, bitch!"

"Willow, please calm down because it ain't that serious," Keena pleaded. "I'm okay, and I've dealt with this fucked up situation. I just want to put this behind us and concentrate on the wedding that will be taking place in two days."

"And I find out two days before my wedding that my nigga and my bitch are keeping secrets from me," Willow replied. "Y'all sholl the fuck right!"

Willow snatched her bag up off the table and headed toward the front door. She needed to go take a timeout because, in the inside, her flesh was burning. She, JD, and Keena made a promise to each other that they would never keep secrets from one another, and this one was major. How could Keena not share her pain with Willow because Keena was right there when Willow lost it all! Keena was the one who stayed up nights with her when Melody got locked up. JD wasn't always around, because he was out hustling trying to make some money so that they could eat. Willow felt devastated, and she wasn't sure if she could forgive Keena for her betrayal. If she hid this from her, then what else could she be hiding?

CHAPTER TWENTY-THREE

"*A*re you nervous about tomorrow?" asked Sam curiously. "Marriage is a big responsibility."

"I was built for this shit!" JD replied arrogantly. "I've been taking care of women since I was a lil' tike. You and Yusuf made sure that a nigga was straight. Speaking of which, he and my mama should have been here by now."

"You found Yanni?" Sam had a surprised look on his face. "Where the fuck was she at?"

"In the Ozarks at a rehab. She ran down there to see Yusuf, and he convinced her to go. It fucked me up when I saw her, and I wanted to hurt her ass!"

"I'm sure, son," Sam offered sympathetically. "The last time I saw her, she was out there bad."

"Well, she don't look bad now," JD, declared. "My mama's looking good! Her skin is smooth and silky like satin once again, and she's healthy. Even her hair is down her back like in the pictures when she was a teenager."

"That's when I fell in love with her. She was younger than me by three years, but I didn't care. I had to have her," Sam admitted. "She was the blackest thang on the block, and them thick ass thighs and her fat ass had all the niggas going crazy." Sam licked his lips and laughed. "I'm glad I left Moni ass at home with the kid."

"I kinda wanted you to bring them. I got a stepmother and a little sister that I've never met, and that's fucked up, Pops. What? You don't want me to meet yo' other lil' family or something?"

"Boy, you something else, JD," Sam uttered and laughed. "I've been telling yo' country ass to come down to Kentucky to meet them. Remember, I invited you to the wedding."

"Yeah, well, I was busy," JD scoffed. "But I can't wait for you to see Yanni."

Willow pulled up behind JD's car that was parked in front of Granny's house. She noticed Sam's truck parked across the street, and KC's car parked behind it. They were supposed to be going to the mall to grab their shoes for the wedding, but Willow was feeling some type of way after her conversation with Keena. The two people that mattered in her life weren't being forthcoming with shit, and she didn't appreciate the disloyalty. She was honest with JD about Locco and was even honest about running to California with Cypher. A part of her felt like she was overreacting and being a drama queen, but the hormonal side of her was pissed, and she felt like arguing with JD's bitch ass because he should have told her about Keena and Cypher.

Willow was about to exit her car when she saw Yusuf's truck turn off MLK Boulevard. A slight smile came across her face because she was happy that he would be a part of their special day. She stepped out of the car and looked into his window as he passed by. There were two women riding with him, and one of them looked like JD's mother, Yanni. She quickly shut the door and rushed into Granny's yard because she wanted to warn JD before Yanni got out of the truck. She ran down the basement steps and turned the knob urgently, bursting through the door.

"Damn, Lil' Baby, what's the matter?" asked JD, jumping up from his seat with his burner in his hand.

"I just saw your uncle Yusuf ride past, and yo' mama is with him!" Willow spat out anxiously. "What hole did he pull her ass up out of?"

"They're here?" JD asked happily. He had a pleasant smile on his face, and it was throwing Willow completely off.

"Nigga, you happy to see her after the way she left yo' ass?" Willow scoffed with a bit of an attitude.

"Chill out, Lil' Baby," JD instructed her. "I saw my mama while I was in the Ozarks, and we made amends. We had a long talk, and I forgave her for leaving me 'cause she checked into rehab and got off dope."

"So, you didn't feel the need share that shit with me when we were in the Ozarks?" Willow questioned. "I mean, damn, nigga, I guess since a bitch about to marry you, you feel like you ain't got to tell me shit now!"

"What the fuck you talkin' 'bout, Lil' Baby?" JD snapped, confused. "My fault for caring more about yo' fucking safety and wellbeing, bi..." Willow narrowed her eyes at JD, and her face drew up into a scowl.

"You were about to call me a bitch!"

"I sure the fuck was, but I caught myself!" JD admitted. "Maybe if you weren't acting like one, then I wouldn't feel compelled to call you one!" Willow was so pissed off because her hormones were out of whack and tears welled up in her eyes. She was already on her way over there to check his ass about keeping secrets with Keena, but now, his mother is back in his life, and he didn't bother to think that. Again, this was something that was important for him to tell her.

"You keeping all these secrets and shit from me, nigga! I wonder if this shit is real between us?" Willow spat, angrily.

"Keeping all what secrets, Willow?" JD asked, frustrated. He was pissed off because Willow was blowing shit out of proportion. "And I ain't finna keep goin' back and forth with yo' ass, 'cause you stressing to my muthafuckin' baby! So, take a few deep breaths, and calm the fuck down, Willow!" This infuriated her even more, and she picked up an open soda can that was sitting on the table and launched it at JD. He ducked, and Sam ran into the next room while Willow continued to pick shit up and throw it at JD.

"Why didn't you tell me that Cypher raped Keena?" Willow shouted. "You knew I would have killed that nigga for violating her like that!"

"I just found out myself!" JD replied. "That's why I was going crazy about you being with that nigga! Yo' ass always going off on the deep end like you're doing now, so that's probably why Keena ain't tell yo' crazy ass! She was trying to save yo' ass from going to jail, but you almost put yo'self there on yo' own!"

"Fuck you, JD!" Willow shouted. "I hate yo' black uglass!"

"So fuckin' what Willow? 'Cause I love your uglass!" JD shot back. He knew that the baby was causing her to act insane, and he was grateful that his Granny had already forewarned him about it. "Calm the fuck down, Willow!"

"What is all this yelling and carrying on going on in my damn basement?" Granny shouted. "You muthafuckas got ya' own house to be arguing and fighting in!"

"Granny, don't nobody want to hear that," JD complained. "This girl down here trippin', and I'm trying to calm her silly ass down!"

"So, I'm silly now 'cause yo' ass hiding stuff from me?" Willow retorted, angrily. "See, I knew this shit was too good to be true! Yo' ass ain't shit like the rest of these niggas out here, and yo' loyalty must be situational, which is some shit I don't need! The fucking wedding is off!"

"BooBoo, I'm here!" Yanni announced, walking down the steps that led into the basement. "I can't wait to see my future daughter-in-law, and I think Yusuf said that it was her who walked into the yard." She walked into the room, and everyone stared at her with varying facial expressions. "I know I was cracked out the last time all y'all saw me, but this bitch is clean and sober now!"

"Yanni, hold up," JD said, sternly. He turned his attention back to Willow.

"Why?" Yanni spat. "I want to see my future daughter-in-law with her pretty self."

"Yanni!" JD shouted. "Shut the fuck up!" Yanni looked at him appalled, but Granny put her hand on Yanni's shoulder and shook her head."

"Now, you care to repeat that shit to me," JD demanded, walking toward Willow. The scowl he wore on his face had all his facial muscles twisted up and distorted. His fists were clenched at his side when he came face to face with her, but it didn't seem to matter because Willow stared him up and down looking unphased.

"I ain't scared of you, JD!" Willow spat. "I said the wedding's off! I don't want to marry yo' black, dusty ass!" She raised her hand and went to take her engagement ring off when JD grabbed her by the wrist aggressively. He squeezed it firmly and stared crazily into her eyes.

"I understand that yo' spoiled brat ass is mad, but you got me fucked up on so many levels, Willow Autumn Shaw! Now, I'll be man enough to admit that I was wrong for not being forthcoming with several things that was going on around us, but my only fucking concern is you and that baby you're carrying in yo' belly. I could give a fuck about Yanni being sober, Keena being raped by Cypher, and that stupid ass nigga, O'Bannon, who keeps sending Patsy's dumb ass over here to get information! My life revolves around securing the bag and making sure shit straight for our future. You're about to start school to follow your dreams, and I'm in school to get my degree in order for us win. So, if you want to get mad a pitch a fit about all this bullshit, then go right ahead and get the shit out of your system. 'Cause one things for certain, and two things are for sure…" JD let Willow's arm go, and he pressed his index finger against her forehead. "You betta have yo' ass here on Saturday at noon so that we can get married, or I'm gon' hunt yo' ass down and kill you myself! You belong to me, Lil' Baby, and don't you ever fucking forget that shit!" He pushed Willow's head back and glared vehemently at her. The look on Willow's face matched his scowl, but her insides were tingling, and her pussy was sopping wet. She wanted to drop to her knees and suck his dick, even though she was furious at him, and that irritated her more than anything!

"Fuck what you talkin' 'bout, playboy," Willow spat. "I guess my ass is dead then, 'cause I won't be here!" She pushed him back in the forehead then ran out the door before he could grab her. He wanted to run after her, but he knew she had to cool down. These blowouts between them were starting to get more serious, and this was something that he definitely didn't want to keep going through with her. They had to come to a better understanding if they intended on making this marriage work.

"So the wedding's off?" Yanni asked confused. Everyone turned to look at her.

"Naw it ain't off," JD answered. "She gone have her ass here tomorrow, 'cause Lil' Baby ain't ready to die."

"JD, you ain't gone kill that girl, so stop talking crazy," Granny ordered, pointing her finger at him. JD tilted his head to the side and looked at her emotionless.

"I don't know why you think I'm playin'. 'Cause I'm killin' that bitch if she don't show up on Saturday, and that's on you, her, and him!" said JD, pointing to his grandmother, mother, and father. "And I mean that shit!"

CHAPTER TWENTY-FOUR

The Next Day

$\mathcal{D}$anni was sitting on the porch watching the traffic go by when she saw JD's Challenger fly past the house. She noticed that the front of the car was damaged, and she wondered why he was driving past the house. Could it be that he missed her and wanted to make amends after that ugly little confrontation she had with Willow? She reached into her pocket and grabbed her cellphone. She dialed JD's number, and it instantly went to voicemail. She called it three more times, and the same thing happened with each call. She knew that he had blocked her, and it angered her. She was the victim in all of this, and she had both the mental and physical scars to show for it.

"Hey, Danni," called out a girl named Chase.

"Hey, Chase! You're up early," Danni mentioned. Chase was a stripper, and she would normally be asleep around this time.

"I got a private party to do tonight, and I have to go shopping to get me something new to wear," Chase explained. "Didn't you use to mess with that nigga, JD? You know he getting married tomorrow to that chick named Willow. His bachelor party is tonight, and he's chartering four party buses full of booze and bitches, and we gone ride through the city. It's gone be so much money being thrown around them muthafuckas that a bitch gon' have all her bills paid for at least three months!"

"You think them broke ass niggas gone spend that type of money?" Danni scoffed, feeling doubtful. "None of those niggas ever looked like they had bread when I was around them."

"I guess JD must have kept you in pocket 'cause them niggas got that bread, bitch! They always coming over to the club making it rain on bitches, and we both know JD ain't broke, so you can stop the fakin'! Ain't ole girl he marrying the one who did that to yo' face?" That statement pissed Danni off, and she jumped up from her chair, feeling embarrassed.

"I was jumped!" Danni shouted. "And don't nobody care about that dusty ass nigga marrying that raggedy ass bitch!" She stormed into the house leaving Chase looking confused. Everyone knew that it was a one on one fight, and Danni got her ass kicked.

Danni slammed the door and stormed into the kitchen. Choppa was sitting at the kitchen table with a few of his boys, but he was on the phone. She snatched open the refrigerator and grabbed one of her coolers. She slammed the door, and it caused Choppa to look over at her in agitation.

"Yeah, Reggie, I got it," Choppa said with a smile on his face. He hung up the phone and directed his attention over to Danni. "I don't know why yo' ass around here slamming shit, but if yo' ass break something, you gone pay for it!"

"Whatever, Choppa," she replied, rolling her eyes. "Don't play with me!"

"What's wrong with you, anyway?" he asked, getting up from the table. "I think I got something that will make you feel better." He walked up to Danni and grabbed her by the waist. He looked down into her eyes and smiled wickedly as he rubbed his finger down her stitches.

"Since you're smiling like that, I hope that means you're finally about to get that bitch together. You promised that she would pay for what she did to my face," Danni whined.

"And I am," Choppa declared. "I just found out that JD and Willow are getting married tomorrow, and their reception is going to be outside on the block."

"How tacky is that! Where are people going to sit?" Danni scoffed.

"According to Reggie, tents are being put up as we speak, and there's a truck with tables and chairs waiting as well," Choppa explained. "That will be the perfect time to crash their wedding and fuck shit up! I'm going to make both they asses regret that they ever ran up in my house!" Danni smiled and wrapped her arms around Choppa's neck.

"I want that bitch dead... You hear me?" Danni asked seductively.

"They both are as good as dead!" Choppa replied. "I promise you!"

✱✱✱✱

O'Bannon was passed out in his bed from the sedative that the doctor had administered. His blood pressure and heart rate had shot up when Patsy had left yesterday, and they weren't able to make it drop down to normal. He was ranting and raving about how Ricky was supposed to be outside guarding his door, but his nurse assured him that Ricky left with Patsy. O'Bannon couldn't believe that both of them were betraying him. Being laid up in a hospital wasn't working for him, because niggas must have forgotten his capabilities. The doctor prescribed a sedative to be administered every eight hours to make sure that O'Bannon got enough rest in order for his body to heal properly. He'd had a minor setback last week due to a complication from his hit and run, so his doctor didn't want anything else to go wrong.

Willow stepped off the elevator hesitantly. She had on a hoodie and made sure that her face was covered as she maneuvered through hallway. She called the hospital and got information regarding O'Bannon's room number by pretending like she was calling from a florist. She was sitting right in front of the hospital when she made the call and typed the information in Notes on her phone before she jumped out of the car.

Willow looked around then slowly pushed the door open; looking behind her to make sure no one saw her entering. She was surprised that Ricky wasn't outside the door, so she figured maybe he was on a cigarette break or something. Either way, she had to move quickly if she wanted to remain undetected. She stood motionless in the middle of the floor when she saw O'Bannon resting peacefully in his bed. He was hooked up to a few machines, and his IV stand had several bags of fluid on it. She noticed that a catheter line was hanging off the side of the bed, and the cast that encased his body looked heavy. Willow didn't feel sorry for O'Bannon because he was about to kill JD if she hadn't run him over. There was one thing that Willow realized the day that she got off the plane in California. She had to kill O'Bannon in order to have any type of peaceful life with JD. Cypher was high on the hit list now that she found out that he raped Keena, but she would take care of him in due time.

Willow eased over to the side of O'Bannon's bed where all the machines were located and studied them for a second. She knew that in order to kill him quietly, she would have to disconnect the alarm to his machine. She wasn't sure how she was going to kill him, but she'd think of something once she handled this first.

"Willow, I'm surprised to see you here," O'Bannon said softly. "Did you finally come to your senses?"

"Shit!" Willow shouted feeling startled. She thought he was sleep, but apparently, he played opossum well. "I thought you were sleep."

"I was sleep, but I just so happened to open my eyes to see you standing here," he replied. "I know you weren't thinking about killing me, Willow. You've already tried that twice and failed both times, so why don't you give it up and give in to my wishes."

"You know I'm an honest bitch, so I will admit that I came here to kill yo' ass," Willow replied sarcastically. "But I guess that wasn't what God had for you, and that's why yo' ass caught me."

"I can hit this little button and call the nurse in here if you'd like," O'Bannon gloated. "I think she'll believe me when I tell her of your intentions, but things don't have to end like that, Willow. You know that I love you more than JD, so why are you trying to pretend like you're in love with him?"

"Because I am in love with him, and we're getting married tomorrow… I guess," Willow admitted.

"It sounds like you're unsure. Baby, I can make you ten times happier, and now that Patsy is going to divorce me, we can concentrate on starting the life that the both of us always wanted together. You can stop all this bullshit with JD, and once the divorce is final, we can get married."

"You're delusional, you know that?" Willow mentioned and laughed. "I was so angry with JD earlier, and the only thing I could think of that would make me feel better about our situation was to kill you. Oh… and this other nigga, but I'll take care of him after the wedding. I'm starting to think that California would be a good place to have a honeymoon." O'Bannon laughed at Willow.

"You have a twisted sense of humor, Willow, but you've always been different. I bet you think I don't know about the shit that you've been doing out in the streets. There's a lot talk about a couple from the Ville that's been terrorizing muthafuckas through the city. Now, I thought this couldn't be you until someone told me about the beat down that you gave some chick that used to fuck around with JD in the laundromat. I never struck you as the jealous type and to hear that you disfigured this young woman over a case of envy because she dated JD was just too much for me."

"Whoever told you that bullshit was a lie, and the truth ain't in them!" Willow snapped. "The bitch tried to cut me up because JD chose me over her, and unfortunately for her, she got her ass kicked. But now that I'm here talking to you, I think letting you live is the better option 'cause my marriage to JD is going to do more harm than killing you." A smug smile came across Willow's face as she walked toward the door.

"You enjoy your last hours of freedom because when you leave, I'm going to call the detective that's handling my case, and I'm going to give him you and that bitch ass nigga's name so the both of you can rot in jail apart!" O'Bannon retorted.

"Do what you feel is necessary, O'Bannon," Willow replied, hunching her shoulders. "I'm about to go get dressed for my bachelorette party, and I hope you have a miserable night!"

"Don't you walk out that door!" O'Bannon shouted as Willow left the room. He wished he could have gotten out of the bed, but it just wasn't possible. He looked over at the machine and noticed his pressure was a bit raised. He took a few deep breaths like the doctor told him and tried to calm down. He laid his head back against the pillow and closed his eyes as he thought about the calming seas of the Atlantic. He planned on taking a trip to the islands when he got out the hospital in order to fully recuperate. He was about to divorce Patsy, and he had a nice settlement coming from it. Also, he had all his hidden drug money that she knew nothing about, so he would definitely come out on top in spite of her intentions.

Sam was hiding in the bathroom when Willow came into the room. He had plans on killing O'Bannon because he didn't appreciate the fact that O'Bannon was trying to kill his son. He knew that JD loved Willow more than life itself, and he'd be damned if he let anyone disrupt his son's happiness.

The door was slightly open, so Sam looked through the crack to see if O'Bannon was up and alert. He had already taken care of the alarm right before Willow came, but he had to run into the bathroom in order to keep her from seeing him. Sam thought Willow was a nurse, but to see that it was his soon to be daughter-in-law made him feel somewhat relieved but, on the other hand, a bit nervous.

Sam calculatedly moved across the floor quickly because he knew he only had one shot to do this. He was ready to do what he did best—kill people for money. But this time, it was a wedding present to his son. Sam had in his gloved hand a handkerchief with some sodium cyanide on it. He planned on putting it over O'Bannon's face, and he would be dead in a matter of minutes.

Sam walked up to O'Bannon's bedside and looked down at him. He went to put the cloth over O'Bannon's nose and mouth, but he opened his eyes up and stared nervously at Sam. He attempted to call out for help, but before a sound was made, Sam had put his deadly hand over O'Bannon's face. O'Bannon only kicked for a second then his body went limp. Sam held his hand in place for an extra minute because he wanted to make sure that the job was done. This nigga wouldn't be causing any more problems for JD and Willow, and Sam's only hope is that Willow's nutty ass showed up for the wedding tomorrow.

CHAPTER TWENTY-FIVE

Later That Night

*I*t was decided that JD and Willow would do a group bachelor and bachelorette party. JD got four party buses for everyone to ride on and made sure there was one for the women, one for the men, one for both men and women, and the additional one for his Granny, Yanni, and Sister Sarah. They got the smaller of the buses, and JD made sure it was full of juice and snacks for them. He put Keena in charge of Willow's bus and told her that she could only have three male strippers on it. Keena laughed because she didn't take JD for the jealous type, but things were changing since Willow was going to be his wife. KC was put in charge of getting the liquor for the three buses and the strippers for JD's bus. He messed around with a stripper chick, so he placed a call to her, and she was bringing a group of the baddest bitches to come represent. KC thought this was a good way to pay homage to JD for being a good mentor and friend to him. If it wasn't for JD, there's no telling how KC's life would have turned out, and he probably would be dead or in jail.

"Three of the buses are already here, and the fourth one is on the way," KC reported. "The strippers should be pulling up in a minute, and I haven't seen Willow since earlier."

"I ain't talked to her ass," JD seethed. "She's probably still pissed off at me and Keena, so she might not show up tonight."

"That'll be fucked up," KC scoffed. "You shelled out a lot of money for tonight, and it would be very selfish of her not to come."

"I don't give four fucks if she doesn't show up tonight, but she better have her funky ass front and center for the wedding tomorrow afternoon!"

"You think Willow would play you like that, JD?" KC asked perplexed.

"Ion know, but I'm gone kill that bitch if she breaks my heart. I promise you that shit!" JD declared. "And that's on Kitchen Crip!"

****

Keena walked up to Willow's door and knocked on it. She waited and counted to ten like she always did then twisted the knob and walked inside. There was music coming from the bedroom and it smelled of their favorite herbal spice. Keena wanted to smooth things over with her best friend because this was supposed to be the kickoff to an epic weekend.

"Willow!" Keena called out. She continued to walk toward the bedroom, nervously. "Willow… are you ready to go?" She walked into the room, and Willow was standing in front of her dressing mirror checking herself over.

"What do you think?" Willow asked with her brow furrowed.

She had on a royal blue strapless dress with the royal blue Jordans on her feet.

"You look cute," Keena gushed. "I'm not surprised that you got on some tennis shoes."

"Girl, that trying to be cute in some heels shit is dead! I plan on partying, so I have to be on firm footing. I can't get drunk, but you hoes better get me high off contact!" Willow scoffed. "JD mixed some hash oil with some Black Afghan together, and I burned it in my oil pot. That muthafucka been smokin', and I've gotten high off contact!"

"We got that handled, bitch. You already know that!" Keena replied, laughing. Willow went back to primping while Keena stared at her uncomfortably. Willow pulled at her curls, trying to get her hair just right. She washed it when she came home then did a twist out and sat up under the dryer. She had to be at the braider early in the morning, so she decided to just do a little something to it. JD requested that she get her hair braided into a feed-in braided bun. She had gotten her hair braided like that before, and he thought it was so flattering for her beautiful face. "Uh... Willow," said Keena, looking down at the floor. "I want to apologize again for not telling you about Cypher. I called myself protecting you, but I ended up doing more damage by not saying anything."

"Look, Keena," said Willow, turning to face her. "It happened, and I'm over it. I hope you've learned not to keep something like that from me, and I promise that we gone get that nigga for what he's done." She walked over to the bed and picked up her gold Rolex watch to complete her jewelry ensemble. She had on a pair of large, gold bamboo earrings in her first hole and a pair of diamond studs in the second one. Keena walked over to the corner on JD's side of the bed. She picked up a t-shirt that was sitting on the floor, and a medium size jewelry box with an orange bow was sitting up under it. She picked up the package then looked over at Willow.

"Your fiancé told me to give you this," said Keena, handing it to Willow. She looked at Keena a bit hesitantly as she took the box from her. Keena watched with anticipation as Willow opened it up, and she smiled when she saw Willow's reaction to her present.

"Oh my fucking God!" Willow shouted, holding up a two-inch-thick Cuban link chain with an iced out charm of his initials. Tears welled up in her eyes as she put it over her head, and let it fall just below her breast. "I guess since I told him I was going to start wearing his chain, he decided to get me one of my own."

"If I'm not mistaken, that's actually his chain," Keena replied. "And please don't hold it against him that he kept my secret. I begged him not to tell you, and he said you were going to be pissed. That boy loves you more than life itself, and you need to stop acting like a hormonal bitch toward him, 'cause I'm the one who gets cursed out when you act like this. He cussed me so bad when you stormed out of the house, that I cried for about thirty minutes. Granny cussed him out for talking to me like that, and Yanni just smoked a thousand cigarettes trying to figure out what she did wrong." Willow laughed as she walked over to her friend.

"I love you, Keena, and thank you for rocking with me! You were in the car with me when I almost killed that nigga O'Bannon, and I promise you that I'm gone get that nigga, Cypher!"

"Fuck his ass! You're about to be Lady JD, so his ass don't matter!" Keena added. "Let's get out of this muthafucka 'cause we got ding-a-ling waiting on us!" She was headed toward the door then stopped and looked at Willow. "Ohhhh... I got ding-a-ling waiting on me 'cause JD said no nigga betta touch you!"

"Fuck what that nigga said!" Willow shouted. "I'm gone grab some dick tonight, and a bitch betta not tell him shit, or I'm gone slap they ass!"

"Enough said," Keena replied frankly. "Let's hit it!"

Keena pulled up behind the last party bus and parked. She and Willow were amped and ready to get involved. JD had given Keena $3,000 in ones to toss out to the strippers. He gave her one strict instruction, and she knew her life depended on it. He told her that none of the male strippers better not put they mouth, dick, or hands on Willow, or he was going to fuck both her and the stripper up. Keena thought it was funny but knew to make sure things stayed PG when it came to Willow. She could grab a little wiener, but the wiener better not grab her back!

The women exited the car and headed up to the bus. Granny was standing outside of the third bus while the male strippers and the few female associates that were invited had already boarded the fourth bus waiting for them. JD and his crew had already taken off because they were ready to get it cracking.

"You getting on this bus with me?" asked Granny, looking pissed.

"No, ma'am," Willow replied. "This is my bus, and I think JD got that bus for you and your friends."

"Me and my two friends like to drink and look at swinging dicks," Granny replied. "It ain't shit like that on this bus, so what the fuck was JD trying to do? I know Yanni is a recovering addict, but who said I wanted to ride around with her square ass!"

"I heard that, Granny!" Yanni yelled out of the window. She came down off the bus and approached the three women standing outside the fourth bus. "I'm no longer getting high, but I like seeing swinging dicks, too!" Everyone started laughing.

"Both of you are more than welcome to get on my bus, but who's going to be on your bus?" Willow asked, shrugging her shoulders.

"Yusuf and my friend, Sarah, can ride on it. He's trying to fuck her, and maybe he'll be able to get there with a private ride around St. Louis," Yanni suggested. "JD put several bottles of champagne in the cooler, so you can give them one of the bottles to drink. I'll get my juice off of that bus, and I promise you don't have anything to worry about with me. I have a whole new lease on life, and I want to be a part of my grandchild's life. JD said that if I go back to being a dope fiend, then I can't be a part of his life, and I don't want to lose my son again. I know that he loves you so much, Willow, and I hope to build a great relationship with you as well." Willow stared Yanni up and down because she wasn't completely sold on it. Willow remembered how it fucked JD up when Yanni disappeared, so she was overly protective of him now that they were getting married.

"Yeah, alright, whatever," Willow uttered. "You just make sure that you don't break my Big Baby's heart again, or else I'm gone fuck you up."

"Oooooohhhhhhhhhh" Keena sang, placing her hand against her mouth. She turned her head and laughed because she couldn't believe that Willow said that to Yanni.

"You just make sure you don't break his heart, missy, or else I'm gone fuck you up!" Yanni shot back. Willow turned her lips up at Yanni then sucked her teeth.

"I doubt that seriously, but whatever," Willow uttered smugly. "I got that nigga on lock, so you don't have to worry, lil' mama. Just remember the only thing you run is your mouth, so don't come around here trying to play mother of the year. We been cool without you, but I'm glad you got your shit together." Willow looked at Yanni and smirked. "Now that we got all of that in order, let's go have some fun!"

CHAPTER TWENTY-SIX

"Girl, I wanna see you twerk. I'll throw all money if you twerk. Ion really think you could twerk. Toot, toot that booty, that big ol' booty. Shake that booty. Can I lay on the booty? Mike Tyson on the booty? Copyright that booty? Toot, toot," rapped JD as he threw money at one of the strippers. Blac Youngsta's joint "Booty" was his jam, and it was beating through the speakers. He told Willow she should walk out to that song at their wedding, and she looked at him like he was stupid. It was going down on his bus, and all the strippers were down to their G-strings, and a few of them were butt ass naked in the back on the pole. KC had set out a pound of Venom OG that he'd gotten from their connect, but everyone was responsible for their own blunts, sheets, and other smoking apparatuses. KC had rolled JD a blunt in a Colombian cigar he'd bought, and it was still burning slowly as JD held it with his lips.

"I got $500 for the best twerker on the bus!" JD shouted. "Now, if your ass or pussy stink, then stay the fuck back! 'Cause if I smell yo' funky ass then I'm gone have the bus driver pull over, and we gone boot that ass off!" Everyone broke out laughing while all the women rushed him and started bouncing and twerkin' their asses at him. JD laughed as he poured champagne all over them and slapped their big ole' butts.

They had been riding around for two hours, and they were good and fucked up! KC had told the bus driver to head to the Riverfront, and they had just pulled down on the strip when KC just so happened to look out the front window and spotted Willow's bus already parked.

"Aye, JD!" KC shouted over the music. "There go Willow's bus parked right there, and Granny's bus is behind it!" JD didn't hear him at first, but then he saw the bus and realized what KC had said.

"Park this muthafucka so I can go see what the fuck Willow is doing," JD ordered. He pushed the women out of his way and walked toward the front of the bus. He tossed the money he was holding in his hand over his shoulder, and the women scrambled to get their share of the bounty. JD wiped his mouth and smiled as the bus came to a halt. His bride to be was pissed at him the last time he'd seen her, but he didn't give a fuck. He was horny ass fuck and wanted to fuck his baby mama 'cause none of these hoes on the bus interested him. JD was loyal as fuck to Willow, and no woman could ever turn his head except his Lil' Baby.

JD climbed off the bus and walked over to Willow's. There were a few people standing outside of it and spoke to him as he made his way up to them. He acknowledged the women dryly and quickly boarded the bus to see what the fuck was going on. "Let Me See It" by UGK was blasting through the speakers, and when he made it to the top of the steps, the first thing he saw was his grandmother getting a lap dance from a buff ass nigga with nothing but a sock on his dick.

"Granny!" JD shouted. "What the fuck you doin'?" Granny gripped the stripper's ass and smiled while JD looked on in horror.

"What the fuck is my granny doing on this bus?"

"What the fuck you doin' on this bus?" Yanni asked, walking up to him.

"I need to be asking you the same damn thing!" JD replied. He looked around and saw his granny's other two friends throwing money at the same stripper that was dancing on her. "Why y'all ain't on the bus I got for y'all?"

"Because we wanted to be where the action was," Yanni scoffed. "I'm a recovering addict, not a born-again virgin! I still like dick a whole lot, and this was the place to be!"

"Where Lil' Baby at?" JD asked looking around Yanni.

"I don't know," Yanni replied. "She probably in the back of the bus with that one stripper that got a big dick!"

"No, the fuck she ain't!" JD shouted. He pushed Yanni over to the side and made his way to the back of the bus. Yanni laughed as her son rush to his fiancée. Willow was sitting over to the side watching Keena get some head from a stripper, and she almost died when he pulled the stripper off Keena and almost punched him.

"What the fuck you doin', JD?" Keena shouted. JD narrowed his eyes as he stared at her. It was dark, and he could barely see. "Willow's uglass is sitting over there!"

"What the fuck you doin' on my bus?" Willow spat.

"I came to get yo' ass," JD replied.

"For what? This our last night of freedom, so go do you so I can keep doin' me!" Willow fussed.

"Shut the fuck up, and come on!" JD demanded. He held his hand out to Willow, and she stared at it like he was diseased. "I'm trying not to call you a bitch, Lil' Baby, so you betta get the fuck up before I snatch you out of that seat!"

"Get the fuck on, JD!" Keena shouted. "You smell like boo-dussy, and my friend don't need to be smelling another bitch's ass and pussy on you!" Willow and Keena burst into laughter, and JD even had to join in.

"Fuck you, Keena!" JD replied, still laughing. "Lil' Baby, come on, 'cause I'm tired of looking at those hoes. My dick is hard, and I want to fuck something."

"You paid for all those strippers, so go fuck one of them," Willow said, waving her hand. "This will be the one and only time that I give yo' ass a pass."

"Ion want it!" JD shouted angrily. Everyone stopped and looked at him. "What the fuck y'all looking at?"

"You, muthafucka!" Granny shouted back. "Now get the fuck up off this bus because you blowing highs!"

"Damn, Granny!" JD complained. His face was frowned up, and everyone laughed at his reaction. "See, Willow, you got my granny clownin' my ass. Why don't you come the fuck on and give daddy some pussy!" He licked his lips then bit down on the bottom one. He was looking so sexy to Willow with his muscles glistening, and his dick print bulging through his grey sweatpants. She noticed his chain with her initials on it, and her ego shot up to 1,000 percent. Willow had a fire contact from all the weed smoking that was going on around the bus, but she would rather go off with her JD because she missed him while she was mad at him.

"Okay," Willow whined, putting up a front. She really wasn't mad, but she pretended to be because she loved when JD showed his feelings. "Do you have any food on your bus because I'm hungry."

"Yo' ass always hungry," JD complained. A smile came across his face, and he leaned over, planting a firm kiss on Willow's lips. "I got you, Lil' Baby, c'mon!"

JD went over to the bus that Yusuf and Sister Sarah were riding on and put them off. He told them to pick one of the other buses to get on because he and his Lil' Baby needed some privacy. Yusuf knew not to argue with JD, so they gathered their things and exited the bus. JD pulled his phone out of his pocket and hooked it up to the auxiliary cord. He pulled up his playlist entitled *My Heart* and pressed play. The first song that came on was his favorite song by Luther Vandross. Each song on the playlist reminded him of Willow, and the song "Forever, For Always, For Love" was his absolute favorite. A warm smile spread across Willow's face as JD sang the lyrics and approached her. He held out his hand, and she placed hers inside of his. The bus driver turned on the disco ball and lights as the couple slow danced to the music. Willow wrapped her arms around his neck, and JD gripped her ass firmly with both hands. They swayed from side to side as Willow's head rested on his shoulder. JD continued to sing the words with such conviction, and Willow felt each and every one of them in depths of her soul. She pulled back and kissed his lips softly, sliding her tongue inside of his mouth. She cupped the back of his head and continued to kiss him passionately as his hands explored her body.

"Drive off," JD ordered the driver as he looked down at Willow. He stepped backward, pulling Willow with him, and he sat down on the bench placing her on his lap.

The bus pulled off playing the next song on the playlist while JD looked seductively at Willow and rubbed his hand up her dress. He pushed her panties over to the side and rubbed his finger against her wet spot. Willow gasped and pressed her lips against his as he plunged his fingers inside of her. They tongue kissed freakily as Willow moaned inside of his mouth.

JD lifted Willow up off his lap and sat her down next to him. He got down on his knees, lifting the bottom of her dress. He never took his eyes off hers, and Willow's pussy got wetter by the second. She pulled down the top of her dress and smiled wickedly as she pinched her nipples. She leaned down and kissed JD's lips while he pulled her panties down to her ankles. She spread her knees, leaning back against the window and played in between her legs while JD watched, licking his lips.

"Move yo' hand, Lil' Baby," JD instructed. "I'm ready to eat."

"Did you say your grace first, nigga? 'Cause I'm tryin' to make sure it's juicy enough for you, Big Baby," Willow moaned. "Just like you like it." She pulled her hands out of her pussy and put them in his mouth. He licked all the wetness off her fingers then plunged his face in between her legs. He pushed his stiff tongue inside the folds of her goodness and worked it in and out like the professional pussy sucker that he was. He licked up her lips and collapsed on her clit. He sucked relentlessly, causing her to moan and groan uncontrollably. She wrapped his ponytail around her hand and pulled whenever he would send a chill down her spine. His head was feeling so good, and she felt her orgasm about to come. A tingling sensation started in between Willow's legs then it spread throughout her body. A euphoric feeling came over her, and she screamed out his name in complete ecstasy.

JD got up off his knees, leaned in, and kissed Willow nastily. She grabbed the top of his grey jogging pants and freed his manhood urgently. She licked around the head and then slid her mouth down the shaft. She bobbed on it a few times then JD pushed her up off of it.

"I don't want no head," JD said firmly. "I want to feel that warm, tight pussy against my dick." He sat down on the bench and pulled Willow on top of him. She lifted her dress up to her waist then eased down on his stiffness.

"Aaaaaahhhhh…" she sighed as his dick filled up her tight womb. She slowly moved up and down on him, but JD had other plans for her. He grabbed her breast and put one of her nipples into his mouth. He flicked his tongue against it then bit down, causing her to gasp. He moved his hand to her hips and pulled her down on his lap, hard. He continued to pound up in her, and Willow just wrapped her arms around his neck and enjoyed the ride. She was loving the dick down because she knew this was his way of making up with her without words being spoken. He pulled her back and stared into her eyes, and they both communicated with one another without saying a word. Willow's pace quickened, so JD knew she was about to cum. He lifted her up and placed her on her back without taking his dick out. He pounded relentlessly inside of her, causing Willow to shake uncontrollably underneath him. She yelled out his name again as her orgasm swept through her body. JD dug down deeper inside of her and pumped a few more times before he came hard in his love spot. He nourished his seed with some protein then he collapsed on top of her when he was done.

"Can we go get something to eat now?" Willow asked, giggling in his ear.

"Whatever you want, Lil' Baby," JD replied then he kissed her lips. "Yo' ass always hungry!"

CHAPTER TWENTY-SEVEN

Wedding Day

JD nervously paced back and forth in Granny's living room. It was almost time for him and Willow to get married, and for some strange reason, he was nervous. They had spent the night in his apartment, and they got up early so she could braid his hair before she left for her hair appointment. Willow had suggested that he get someone else to do it, but he insisted that she did it. They made love in the shower, which made her late. As usual, JD didn't give a fuck, so Willow didn't either.

"Has anyone talked to Willow?" JD asked anxiously.

"I talked to Keena, and she said Willow's at the house getting ready now," Granny assured him. "Apparently, she arrived at the braiders late, so it completely threw the time off."

"I wonder what made her late," Sam added sarcastically. He stayed in JD's spare room while Yusuf, Yanni, and Sister Sarah stayed at Willow's apartment. All of them stayed up very late and partied into the wee hours when JD and Willow arrived back at the house. "I heard some moaning and groaning coming from the bathroom eeeaaaarrrlllyyy this morning!" Sam implied. JD looked over at his father with a smirk on his face.

"Yeah, I fucked her this morning," JD replied shamelessly. "That's our morning routine."

"That's why her belly's full," Granny added. "I hope y'all don't sit up and have a bunch of kids. The two of you need to enjoy being married before you complicate your life with a bunch of kids."

"I plan on having ten nappy headed babies with my Lil' Baby, so you better get ready for it, Granny," JD replied arrogantly. "But I hope their hair take after mine!"

"I hope you don't think I'm gone keep all those nappy headed lil' fuckers," Granny shot back. "This ole gal ain't got the patience for it, so you gone have to look elsewhere to find a babysitter!"

"I'll gladly watch my grandbabies," Yanni gushed. "And I'm going to love all over them."

"We gon' watch our own kids, so don't nobody have to worry about it," JD stated frankly. "Willow just needs to get her ass together so we can get this shit over with!

****

Willow came out of the bedroom looking stunning in her wedding dress. It was a white lace, open back strapless gown with a sweetheart neckline and mermaid bottom. It flowed down to the floor and you couldn't see her shoes up under it.

"Damn, bitch! You look amazing!" Keena gushed. "I'm feeling jealous as a muthafucka!" Willow looked at her bestie and smiled.

"Bitch, you look cute too!" Willow replied. Keena had on a royal blue satin dress that was form fitting at the top with spaghetti straps, and it belled out at the bottom, stopping at her knee. Here royal blue Chuck Taylors with orange shoelaces matched the pair Willow had on under her dress, and the rest of the wedding party would be wearing them. Both JD and Willow carried their hood love deep, and they wanted to incorporate it into their wedding without overdoing it. "I'm so nervous," said Willow, walking over to the long mirror that hung on the closet door. "Bitch, I'm about to marry JD. Can you believe it?"

"Yes, I can believe it!" Keena admitted. "The two of you were destined to be together!" Keena's text message ringtone went off, and she looked down at the phone.

JD: Tell Willow to hurry the fuck up! I'm getting tired of waiting!

Keena laughed because this was classic JD. "Yo' man said, 'hurry the fuck up 'cause he's tired of waiting.'"

Willow lifted an eyebrow and turned up her lips.

"His ass was the reason why I'm running late! He insisted that I braid his hair for the wedding. Plus, we fucked this morning in the shower, and that took up an hour."

"That baby's got your hormones going crazy, huh?" Keena asked nosily.

"Girl! A bitch stays wet like a fresh mountain spring," Willow replied, laughing. "JD says he could just leave his dick inside of me for days, and it doesn't have to be on hard."

Sam walked through the door and stopped when he saw Willow in her dress. He was speechless because she looked breathtaking. His son was lucky to find a bride that loved him just as much as he loved her, and Sam knew that the two of them would have a wonderful life together.

"Willow, you look so beautiful," Sam declared. "My son is a lucky man."

"I'm with you when you're right," Willow replied, laughing. "That nigga's damn lucky to have me!"

"You have no argument coming from me," Sam added. "However, his impatient ass has sent me to get you." Willow and Keena laughed.

"That nigga's just ready to get drunk and party," Willow scoffed then laughed. "I'm ready to leave, though. I just need to grab my bouquet." She walked over to the bed and picked a bouquet of white lilies wrapped with silver, royal blue, and orange ribbon. Sam did a double take when she also picked up a chrome 9-millimeter pistol with an ivory handle.

"Where are you going with that?" Sam asked confused. Willow smiled brightly as she handed Keena the flowers. She went over to the dresser and grabbed a white double shoulder holster that was decorated with rhinestones. She put the pistol in one of the holsters and grabbed another, putting it in the other.

"I'm ready to go," Willow announced cheerfully.

"Why do you have on a shoulder holster with pistols in them?" Sam asked again, feeling perplexed. Willow looked at him confused.

"JD wanted me to wear these," Willow stated proudly. "He bought me these as a wedding gift, and he even had our initials engraved on the handle in gold. He has a set too, but my name is engraved on the barrel of each one of his." Sam stared at her strangely.

"The two of you are insane." Sam laughed. "I have never seen no shit like this, but I have to remember both of you are young gangstas."

"We got enemies in these streets, so we're prepared for any haters who might want to come around here and be petty muthafuckas. Both JD and I had a bad feeling this morning, and if my baby say strap up, then a bitch gon' strap up! Now, you ready, Pops, 'cause my Big Baby is waiting for me." Keena handed Willow her flowers and smiled at Sam. She lifted up her dress to expose the waist holder she had on with a .25 caliber pistol in it.

"Y'all too gangsta around this muthafucka!" Sam laughed, holding out his arm. Willow picked her small purse up off the dresser then walked over to Sam with a bright smile on her face. She linked her arm around it, and they started out the room so she could go marry her best friend. Willow was nervous, but she was ready to start her beautiful life with JD.

****

Cypher was headed down MLK toward Willow's hood because he had to talk to her. He was out on bond for manslaughter, and he wanted to tell Willow what happened to him, thinking that maybe she would feel sorry for him and take him back. The GPS told him to make a left onto Billups Avenue, but he couldn't because it was blocked off. There were some men standing on both sides that were turning people away. Cypher eased down the street and pulled into Martin's Convenience Store lot. He saw a man and woman, who were dressed up, coming out of the store with a bag, so he figured they might know what was going on. He put the car in park and jumped out of the car.

"Excuse me," Cypher said, walking up to the couple.

"What's up?" the man asked, staring at him strangely.

"Why is that street blocked off?" Cypher asked, pointing toward Billups Avenue.

"JD and Willow are about to get married," the woman said happily. The man she was with glared at her.

"It's a private reception, playboy," the man offered. "C'mon." He walked off and the woman followed him. Cypher stared down the street with a stupid look on his face. He quickly opened up his car door and jumped inside of it. He picked up his phone and dialed Willow's number with urgency, but the voicemail picked up on the first ring. Cypher panicked and dialed it again, but the same thing happened. He slammed his fist on the steering wheel and shouted out a few fucks. He went to his text messages and found the one with her address on it. He punched it into the GPS and found that it was only a few blocks away from where he was sitting. He put his foot on the brake and pushed the button to start the car. He put it in drive and took off out of the parking lot like a bat out of hell. He almost hit a car in oncoming traffic, but he didn't give a fuck! The only thing on his mind was finding Willow, and he hoped that he wasn't too late.

CHAPTER TWENTY-EIGHT

$\mathcal{S}$am opened the front door and held it while Willow walked out of it. She was holding the bottom of her dress up, so it wouldn't get dirty by dragging on the ground, and Keena came out behind her holding it from the back. She was just as excited about the day as the couple, and she couldn't wait to see JD's face when Willow walked into the room.

"Willow!" a voice shouted. "Willow, wait!" Both Willow and Keena started looking around because they didn't know where the shouting was coming from. A White Rolls Royce was sitting in front of the house waiting to take her down to Granny's, so no cars could turn on the block or get past.

"Willow, get in the car," Sam instructed, but she stopped, paralyzed from the sound of Cypher's voice, and she wanted to make sure she wasn't tripping.

"Okay," Willow uttered. She went to walk down the steps when Cypher came running up the lawn and stopped in front of her.

"You look so beautiful!" Cypher said, staring at her in awe. "Please don't marry JD! He can't take care of you or love you like me!"

"Who is this nigga," said Sam, trying to move around Willow and Keena. Willow tilted her head to the side and dropped her flowers to the ground in disbelief. She reached over her bosom and grabbed the handle of one of her pistols. She pulled it out and slapped Cypher across the face with it making him fall back down the steps. She rushed down behind him with Keena still holding the back of her dress. She switched hands and grabbed the barrel of the gun then hit Cypher again upside his head with the butt of it. She continued to swing calculatedly, hitting him viciously while Keena stomped him in the head.

"Bitch ass nigga, you got a lot of nerve showing yo' face around here after you raped my best friend, my muthafuckin' sister!" Willow shouted. She and Keena continued to beat him down while some of their homeboys ran up to see what was going on. Sam tried to grab Willow, but she pushed him back and continued unleashing her fury on Cypher.

"Aaaahhhh!" Cypher continued to call out in pain. "Willow, please! I can explain! She's lying! She's lying!"

****

"JD! JD!" KC shouted, busting into Granny's house.

"Nigga, what's wrong with you busting up in my Granny shit like you crazy or something!" JD yelled with a scowl on his face.

"My bad, but Willow's up the street fighting some nigga!" KC replied out of breath. "Sam down there trying to break it up, but both Willow and Keena are out there getting loose!"

"Fuck!" JD shouted, dropping his suit jacket to the ground. Yanni gasped when she noticed the double shoulder strapped holster he was wearing with two big guns in it. "Let's go!" he said, running toward the door.

"Where you goin'!" Yanni shouted, running behind him.

"To go get my bitch!" he replied, running out the front door. He skipped down the steps and leaped on the short brick wall Granny had behind her fence and jumped over it. He took off running through the tents and tables headed toward the house. He didn't know who the fuck this could be, but whoever it was made a fatal mistake trying to fuck up his wedding day.

JD was hitting it down the street when he heard two shots ring out in the direction he was headed. His heart dropped in his stomach because he hoped it wasn't his Lil' Baby that was shot. He continued to run up the block with Willow in sight. He felt a little better, but rage filled his body 'cause someone was fucking with Willow!

"What the fuck is going on!" JD shouted as he ran up.

"This bitch ass nigga gone lie and say he didn't rape Keena!" Willow yelled in rage. "He violated by coming here and fucking up our wedding day, but then this nigga gone add insult to injury!" JD looked down and saw Cypher lying on the ground bleeding from his head and leg.

"Did you shoot him, Lil' Baby?" JD asked, frowning at Cypher.

"Naw! Keena shot that bitch ass nigga!" Willow shot back. She spit on Cypher then stomped on the leg he was shot in. "Bitch ass nigga!"

"Willow, chill the fuck out before you get blood on your wedding dress!" JD ordered. "You look beautiful, Lil' Baby, and I don't want you to fuck it up. Gone back in the house, and I'm gon' handle it." Willow stared at him angrily because she wasn't trying to hear shit he was talking about.

"I'll go up on the steps, but I ain't going in no fucking house!" she declared. JD glared at her for a second with a look of death.

"Give me a kiss," he demanded. Willow leaned forward and pressed her lips firmly against his. "You ready to marry me, Lil' Baby?"

"Nigga, don't ask me no stupid ass question like that," Willow spat. "Don't you see me? Don't I look like I'm ready to marry you?"

"First of all, you betta check ya tone 'cause you the one down here wildin' out on a nigga when you was supposed to be on yo' way up the street to marry me. Second of all, you got my dick hard as a muthafucka, and I was about to take you in there and bend yo' ass over before we made our way down to Granny's house to get married." Willow's face softened, and a slight smile danced on her lips.

"Nigga, you wasn't gon' get no pussy. I'm sorry," Willow confessed. "I'm not coming up out this dress until tonight when we christen our marriage." She reached up and kissed his lips again.

"What you want to do with this nigga?" JD asked.

"You better send that nigga to the hospital, and let his ass gone on about his business," said their friend, Nikki. "That nigga was all over the internet for shooting and killing some nigga in his house!"

"They was trying to rob and kill me, Willow," Cypher cried. "Indigo is in the ICU hanging on to her life, and she's pregnant! Charisma set me up, and his cousins tried to kill me!"

"What!" Keena shouted, shocked. She knew that Charisma promised to handle Cypher, but damn! She just thought he was going to get him beat up real bad.

"I don't give a fuck!" Willow snapped. "Chino, take that nigga to the old man, and tell him I said to patch this bitch nigga up. Get the fuck up off the ground!" Cypher stood up, wiping the blood from his eye. He could barely stand because of the bullet in his leg.

"Thank you, Willow," Cypher sniffled. "I love you, and I'm sorry for everything that I've done to ever make you hate me! I know that's my ba—" JD punched Cypher in the face, knocking him out cold.

"Take this bitch ass nigga on out of here!" JD ordered. "Better yet, tell old man I said make sure that nigga stays sleep for a few hours, and someone will be by to get his ass later. How did that nigga get here anyway?"

"That's his rental car sitting in the middle of the street behind the Rolls," said Nikki pointing at it. "It's still running, too!"

"Search that nigga's pockets and take the car with you. Park it in front of the old man's house and keep the keys. It's a rental car, so it won't look out of place," JD instructed.

"C'mon, Daddy," said Willow, wrapping her arms around JD. "Let's go get married!" He looked at her and smiled.

"You's a muthafucka, you know that?" JD asked, laughing. He placed his hand on the side of Willow's face then pressed his lips firmly against hers. "Let's go."

****

JD stood nervously as Willow walked toward him, Sam, and the minister. "Forever, For Always, For Love" by Luther Vandross was playing, and both Willow and JD were singing the words softly to themselves as she approached the arch decorated with her favorite flowers. They stared lovingly into each other's eyes as they both sang the words,

"I'd be a fool to ever change if she said she loves the way I am. I'd be a fool to ever change if she said she loves the way I am. It's gonna be starting here, starting now. Yeah, yeah, yeah. Forever, for always, for love." The music slowly leveled off to a low tone and played in the background. JD took Willow's hand into his and lifted it to his lips. He placed a soft kiss on the back of it, and she smiled bashfully at her man. Everyone laughed and commented as they stared at each other goo-goo eyed. It was like they were seeing each other for the first time, and they both were anxious to get this shit over.

The service flowed smoothly, and the minister got to the part where he asked for any objectors. Both Willow and JD put their hand on one of their guns and looked around the room with serious mugs on their face. Everyone in the place fell out laughing, and even the minister made a comment about how both of them *Punk'd* the entire room. He continued the ceremony, and they presented each other with their rings. The large marquise cut diamond was attached to a diamond-studded band. He switched out the rings that he got her at first because he wanted it to be a surprise when he presented it to her. She placed a diamond-studded band on his finger, and then they presented each other with the Cuban link chains with each other's initials on it. Their nuptials were like a comedy show, and the both of them provided plenty of one-liners that kept the crowd laughing the entire ceremony. They finally made it to the kiss, and JD dipped Willow down when he slid his tongue into her mouth. They kissed for several seconds while everyone cheered and catcalled. He stood Willow up and kissed her lips quickly one more time before he turned to greet everyone with his new bride. Willow was so happy that she was finally Mrs. Julio Delgado. Her face was glowing, and that meant everything to JD because all he wanted to do was make her happy. He devoted his life to her and made a promise that he would dead anything that opposed their happily ever after!

CHAPTER TWENTY-NINE

The Reception

$\mathcal{T}$he reception was lit! Granny ended up getting a friend of hers that catered to handle the food for the wedding. They had a full spread of fried chicken, baked chicken, barbecue chicken, Swedish meatballs in sauce and out of sauce, beef ribs, mostaccioli, pasta con broccoli, green beans, corn, sweet potatoes, mash potatoes, tossed salad, Greek salad, dinner rolls, and croissants. The dessert table consisted of all types of pound cake, cake pops, candy apples, three types of cookies, and the wedding cake. They had people serving the food, and you could go back as many times as you'd like. It was a b.y.o.b affair, but JD had a champagne fountain that was flowing Moet, and there were plenty of bottles being popped at the affair by the guest. Everyone was happily eating and drinking as they celebrated the union of their hood king and queen.

"Are you happy, Lil' Baby?" JD asked, smiling warmly at his bride.

"Yes, baby," she replied and kissed his lips quickly. "This is better than I ever imagined!"

"I'm glad, and there's more to come," JD assured her. "We're going on a honeymoon to Las Vegas tomorrow morning, and when my passport comes back, we're leaving this muthafucka. You can pick anywhere on the map, and we're going!"

"That sounds wonderful," she gushed. "You are my everything, Julio Delgado!" She leaned in and kissed his lips passionately as Sam approached them.

"Save that for the honeymoon!" Sam shouted, teasing the both of them. "Cut that shit out!"

"Leave them alone," Yanni demanded, pushing Sam on the shoulder. "They just got married, and it was a beautiful ceremony!"

"More like *Def Comedy Jam: Wedding Edition*," Sam joked. Willow stopped kissing JD and laughed with both of them.

"Get the fuck on, Sam," JD laughed. "Y'all got me and my Lil' Baby fucked up!"

"Both you and your Lil' Baby are fucked up!" Sam rebutted. "Look at both of you sitting here strapped up at your wedding. You're supposed to have your guys posted to make sure don't no shit pop off."

"We got niggas posted, Sam," JD assured him. "But a nigga can never be too careful."

"Anyone can be touched," Willow added.

"Now, if you'll excuse us," JD said, standing to his feet, "me and my Lil' Baby need to go thank our guests for attending." He held out his hand, and Willow placed hers inside of his. He helped her up out of her seat and kissed her shoulder gently.

"You used to love me like that," Yanni uttered, reminiscing as JD and Willow walked past them.

"I used to love you like JD loves Willow, but that was a long time ago," Sam replied. "I'm glad you're getting your life together, and you look good, girl!"

"Thank you," said Yanni bashfully. "It's funny how you can still make me blush." Sam looked around then walked closer to Yanni. He pulled her to him then whispered in her ear.

"I can do a lot more than that," he whispered. "But it's only if you want to." He pulled away and looked at Yanni seductively. Sam was still fine as ever, and her pussy was dripping just thinking about fucking him.

"Okay, let's go!" she agreed with a big smile on her face. Sam put his arm around her waist, and they disappeared out of sight.

JD and Willow were on their way to greet their guest when Keena made them go have their first dance. She planned the perfect song for them, and she wouldn't tell them what it was. All she kept saying is go over to the dance floor and get ready. She cued the DJ, and Troop's song "I Will Always Love You" came booming out of the speakers. The three Amigos, JD, Willow, and Keena, fell out laughing because this song held a special meaning to all of them. Whenever Yanni and Sam had one of their marathon fucking sessions, the song would continuously play on repeat in Yanni's room. JD would always come outside complaining about it and vowed that one day he was going take the CD and break it into several pieces. He never got a chance to do it because Yanni beat him to the punch. She got mad at Sam one day and broke the cd in his face when they finally broke up for good.

The couple finished their dance then went around greeting their guests. They thanked everyone for coming, and several of the people in attendance handed them cards and wads of cash. There were all walks of life in attendance at their reception, but people had to have an invitation in order to attend. They had homeboys posted at all the key places that let people in and out of the area. The couple walked over to Granny to give her some of their bounty, and Willow sat down next to her because she needed to stop for a minute.

"I need to take a break, JD," Willow said, fanning herself. "I'm gone sit here with Granny, so you can go over there and smoke with KC and them."

"Maybe I want to stay over here with you and Granny. It ain't like yo' ass don't always be up under me." He looked down at her smugly. "I guess yo' ass don't like it, huh?" Willow cut her eyes at him, and they both laughed.

"Boy, if you don't take your ass over there, and get out of my face!" Willow spat, pointing in the direction of his homeboys. "I'm gone—"

"You gon' what?" JD questioned with a frown on his face. Willow lifted an eyebrow at him.

"Now, you know good and damn well when you look at me like that my pu—" Willow looked over at Granny. "Ewww, Granny! I done forgot you were sitting here! JD go play with your friends for a minute before you make me embarrass myself in front of Granny!"

"You're already there," JD called out and laughed. He kissed Willow's lips quickly then walked off to go hang with his boys for a few minutes. Willow watched her man proudly as he strutted across the street because he looked so sexy in his slacks with the suspenders. Black niggas looked fire in all white, and her man looked too fine in his dressy attire. He wore a mean gangsta lid (hat) on some of their wedding photos, and the photographer got a kick out them pulling their guns and taking a few shots like the gangstas in the movies from the 40's and 50's."

"I'm so happy for the both of you," Granny gushed. "I told you that he was your husband, and I'm glad you took heed to it." Granny patted Willow's hand and smiled. "Now, who was that you were fighting around the corner before the wedding?" Willow looked at her shamefully then held her head down.

"Granny, it was Cypher. Apparently, he'd gotten into some trouble in California, and he came running to me for help like I did when I hit O'Bannon with JD's car," Willow explained.

"Speaking of O'Bannon," Granny said solemnly. "Patsy called me late last night crying hysterically. She said they found O'Bannon dead in his hospital bed. They don't know what happened, but somehow, he suffocated." Willow looked at Granny. She was spooked because she had gone there earlier that day to kill him.

"Do they think he was murdered?" Willow stammered. "I mean how does a person suffocate?"

"We gon' call it an act of God and leave that shit alone," Granny declared. "Let that muthafucka rot in hell, and you focus on being a good wife and mother to JD and that baby you're carrying." Granny wrapped her arms around Willow and squeezed her tightly. Willow hugged her back and smiled as she watched JD laugh and clown with his friends. She noticed a man wearing all red walking toward JD, and when he raised up a gun and fired several shots at her husband, she sprang to her feet, drawing both guns from their holster. She took off running in their direction as she watched JD fall to the ground. Several people stood in shock while others began running and screaming in all directions. Willow continued toward the action, but she didn't fire because there were too many people around. She watched as the man in all red tried to make his way to the barricade, and she turned to follow him because there was no way she was letting his ass get away. KC and a few other homeboys were right behind her with their guns in hand, but no one fired because, again, there were too many innocent people running around them.

Willow made it to the barricade and held up both of her guns. She started letting off shots as she continued to chase the man down the street. KC ran passed her and continued to fire because Willow had run out of bullets. She didn't break her stride and continued to truck up the street because she was determined to catch the nigga. The man in red turned down North Market Avenue, and by the time he made it to the end of the block, he got hit with a car by one of the homeboys. Both KC and Willow made it down to him at the same time, and he laid squirming on the ground crying out in pain from the injuries he'd suffered. Willow snatched KC's gun out of his hand and cocked back the hammer.

"Who the fuck sent you?" she asked, placing the gun to his head. "Who the fuck sent you!"

"Bitch, you know who sent me!" the man spat back. "Choppa

and Danni said congratulations on your marriage!" He spat blood on Willow's dress, and it sent her over the edge. She held out the gun and unloaded the last of the bullets in his head and throughout the rest of his body. KC grabbed the gun out of her hand and quickly opened the car door. There were people around, but Willow didn't give a fuck! No one better not open up they mouth, or they would meet the same fate as that this bitch nigga lying dead on the pavement. KC pushed Willow into the back seat and jumped in behind her. Willow's only concern was getting back to JD because she didn't know how badly he was hit.

CHAPTER THIRTY

*J*D slowly opened his eyes to a bright, hazy blur of lights. He was in some pain, but his memory was a bit foggy. He remembered looking into the eyes of a random stranger

then being shot. His vision began to resurface, but reality hit him when he heard the beeps of machines and saw all the tubes and IVs that were hooked up to his body. He turned to his right, and there, by his bedside, was his wife. His hand was enclosed in hers, and she lay quietly sleeping by his side. Lil' Baby looked so angelic as he listened to her soft snore. Why the fuck would someone come for him on their wedding day? He had a feeling that something was going to happen, but getting shot wasn't what he expected. The last thing he remembered was watching Willow run after the dude in red and him mumbling that somebody needs to watch her back. After that, everything else was a blur, but it was evident that he'd gotten fucked up. JD knew that the best thing to do right now was to heal his body and concentrate on keeping his wife and unborn child safe. This was the first time Sampson was down, but Delilah had his back, and she was going to make sure her man was whole again.

JD wanted to wake Willow up, but he couldn't talk due to the tube in his throat. It was already aggravating him, and he'd just woken up, so the first thing he needed to do was get someone to remove it. It was scratching his throat, and he just didn't want the shit on him. He slid his hand from up under Willow's, and she instantly jumped up with a pistol in her hand. She looked around the room in killer mode then placed her eyes on JD. He smiled at Lil' Baby with his eyes, and her face softened as a single tear ran down her face. JD reached up and wiped it before he placed his hand on her cheek. Willow instantly grabbed it then kissed his palm as more tears continued to flow.

"I thought I lost you," Willow cried softly. "You were shot four times—once in your left shoulder, twice in the side, and once in your left arm. You were lucky because none of your organs were hit. However, the doctors had a bit of difficulty getting one of the bullets out of your side. It was the only one that didn't go straight through, and it was lodged near your kidney." JD pointed to the tubing in his mouth and widened his eyes. A slight smile came across Willow's face because she knew exactly what he wanted. "You want to get that tube out of your mouth?" He nodded his head and softened his eyes. He was glad that Willow wasn't a stupid bitch, and she was able to understand him with just a hand movement and eye contact. "Let me buzz the nurse to let her know that you're awake."

Willow walked around his bed and pressed the button. JD noticed that she had his suit jacket on, but when she turned to come back around on the other side, he noticed that the front of her dress was covered in blood. He continued to study her, and with further scrutiny, he realized the impact of what happened. Their wedding day will forever be plagued with the fact that he'd been shot up at their reception, and Willow had to suffer through not knowing if he was going to live or die.

"Willow, now that JD's up, why don't you go home, take a shower, and change clothes?" Yanni suggested. Willow looked at her crossly.

"I'm not going anywhere!" Willow replied. "If you're that concerned about my appearance, why don't you go buy me something to wear, and I can take a shower here at the hospital."

"I didn't mean it like that, Willow," Yanni replied defensively. "I'm just as concerned for you as I am for my son. I saw the way you took off running after that man with no hesitation with both pistols in hand, and I realized in that moment why my son loves you so intensely. If it was me, I would have run over to JD, but you took the initiative to go after the muthafucka that did this to my baby." Tears streamed down Yanni's face, and Willow put her hand on her mother-in-law's shoulder.

"I'm sorry for just being a bitch toward you," Willow apologized. "We're all under a lot of stress, but the good thing is JD is alright. I don't know what I would have done if JD had died. However, I promise you that I'm going to get every last one of those muthafuckas that's involved!"

"They said the guy who shot up JD is dead," Yanni mentioned casually.

"I know," Willow replied smugly. "Because I'm the one who killed him." She looked Yanni square in the eyes with an intense gaze and lifted an eyebrow. "Now, if you'd excuse me, I need to kiss my husband because I'm so glad that he is alive." A small smile danced around the corners of Willow's lips, and she walked intently over to JD's bed.

"KC is out beating the pavement trying to get more information on who put this hit out on you," Sam explained, studying his son. The nurse had just left from taking the breathing tube out of JD's mouth, and he felt relieved.

"KC ain't out looking for shit," JD replied slowly. "That nigga's at the crib getting shit ready for when I touch down. We know who the fuck did this, and that bitch ass nigga and that dusty ass hoe gone pay for what the fuck they did to me!"

"You fucking right!" Willow interrupted. She brushed her hand across JD's forehead then placed a kiss in the center of it. "I killed the nigga that shot you up, Big Baby, and I'm going to go handle the other two muthafuckas that did this weak ass shit to you! They were too cowardly to do it themselves, so they sent another weak ass nigga, but they didn't know that Lil' Baby always has her husband's back, and I handle his ass like I was supposed to. 'Til death do us part, Mr. Delgado." JD and Sam stared at Willow admirably.

"'Til death do us part, Mrs. Delgado," he replied.

"KC is already up on shit, and he's just sitting back waiting for me to give him the word. Keena had got hit in the arm, but they fixed her right up, and she was able to go home."

"Did I hear my name?" asked Keena, walking through the door. She had a cast on her arm, and she slowly made her way over to the bed. She had Willow's Gucci carry-on bag in her hand, and it looked like it was filled to capacity. "Nigga, y'all had the most epic reception in history! Muthafuckas won't let y'all ass be great, and the hate is fucking real!"

"Ain't that the fucking truth!" Willow agreed. "The happiest day of my life turned into the scariest day of my life, but I'm thankful to God that he spared my king! Half of the West Side would be burned down by now, and I wouldn't have stopped until Choppa and Danni were dead!"

"This insane girl took off running with both her pistols in her hand after the lil' nigga that shot you," Sam mentioned and laughed. "I see why y'all asses got married now. Both of y'all are equally psychotic, and Willow's nuttiness definitely matches yours, son!"

"This my Lil' Baby," JD gushed with a slight smile on his face. "And I know if don't know other muthafucka got my back, she most definitely does without no hesitation!"

"You got that shit right, Big Baby," Willow declared. She leaned down and kissed his lips firmly. She sucked on his bottom lip for a second then pulled away with a frown on her face. "Where is the Vaseline? Your lips are dry as hell, baby!" Everyone started laughing as Willow looked around the room. It was full of people that cared for him, but the only person that was missing was Granny. She refused to come to the hospital after seeing his bloody body laid out in the middle of the street.

"I brought you a few outfits and some underwear. I know you're not leaving the hospital until JD is released, so I made sure that you're set for a few days at least. I'll be up at this muthafucka every day, so I can take the dirty clothes home with me and bring you more when I come," Keena explained. "I got y'all back, so don't worry about nothing."

"Thanks, ugly," JD joked. "My Lil' Baby is going to need your help, and I appreciate you being here, sis."

"I'm glad that you're here with us, bruh! We weren't sure if we'd lost you, but Willow held it together like the good wife. She refused to let you die, and she even threatened to die just to find you and kill you again!" Keena joked. Everyone laughed as Willow shook her head in agreement.

"I did say that," Willow admitted. "Yo' ass wasn't about to leave me with no baby and a lot of anger issues."

"There's no way I was leaving you and our son," JD declared. "No one or nothing is going to stop us, Willow. I'm still going to give you the beautiful life that I promised you, and we're not going to have to worry about anyone who opposes us."

"'Til death do us part," Willow uttered. She leaned down and kissed his lips again because she was so grateful to God that JD's life was spared.

Later that night, JD was moved to a private room. Willow took a shower and changed clothes after wearing her husband's blood on her for two days. He didn't wake up until later the next day after he'd been shot, and Willow refused to take off her wedding dress because she wouldn't leave JD's side. She was going to wear his blood like a coat of armor because, at the time, his fate wasn't known. Also, if JD were to die, Willow wanted to be in her wedding dress because it would symbolize her undying love for her husband. Speaking of which, Willow refused to get in bed with him after the nurse explained the importance of not lying on or getting entangled in his IV line. He didn't give a fuck about what the nurse said and even threatened to get out of his bed to come get in hers if she didn't do what he said. He told Willow that he's the head of their household, and she'd better get used to taking orders. Willow pulled out her pistol and held it up in the air, and a big smile spread across JD's face. She walked over to his bed and placed it under the pillow before she nestled up next to him. He wrapped his arm around her waist and rested his hand on her belly. This was where it normally rested each and every night when they laid down to go to bed, and tonight would be no different, except that they were married, and their happily ever after was about to begin.

CHAPTER THIRTY-ONE

Six Months Later

"*J*'m going to give you ten seconds, Willow," said JD, looking down at his watch.

"I don't think I'm going to need that," she replied smugly. KC looked at both of them and laughed.

"Let's get it!" Sam suggested, and Willow kicked in the door. They were dressed in bulletproof vests and heavily armed with assault rifles and pistols. Both JD and Willow opted to use their matching guns to handle the business at hand. After a lot of careful planning and intimidation, they had finally got the location to where Choppa and Danni were hiding out. They had been laid up at a house that Choppa owned out in North County that he shared with his wife, Whitney. She found out that Choppa had been playing house down in the city with Danni, and the static that he had with JD was stemming from that bitch. Well, Whitney flipped her lid, to say the least. She moved her and the children's stuff out of the house and had plans to file for a divorce. In the process of her telling a few people about her sudden heartbreak, the information fell on the ears of a thot that just so happened to be the sister of the murderous couple, Mr. and Mrs. Delgado. Keena couldn't call Willow fast enough with the whereabouts of Choppa and Danni, and Willow couldn't share the information fast enough with her husband. This day was carefully planned down to the last dead body that would drop, and you know who would be doing the killing. Sam and KC had strict instructions to just provide coverage because JD and Willow were going to provide the extermination.

They quickly made their way into the house with Willow in the lead. JD followed quickly behind her with KC covering him and Sam bringing up the rear. The house was two stories, and it was 3:00 a.m., so they figured that the couple was upstairs in bed. Willow hit the steps two at a time, making her way to the top. She had both guns up in the air next to her ears as she leaned against the wall and checked the area. She waved JD and the rest of the crew up, and they proceeded to follow behind Willow as they headed to the bedroom. KC and Sam checked the rooms before they proceeded forward. All of them were empty, so that meant that Choppa and Danni were right behind the closed door in front of them. There was music coming from behind it, and the R&B slow jam that was playing let them know what was probably going on.

Willow looked back at JD and smiled devilishly at him while she mouthed the words to Beyonce's song "All Night Long." The song was ironic because it embodied everything that represented their love for each other. She moved back down toward JD and kissed his lips passionately. She slid her tongue inside of his mouth, and they made out to the rhythm of the music playing in the background. Their bodies weren't touching, yet they were one at the mouth. Their adrenaline filled bodies were feeling both lust and passion from the job that faced them at hand. Behind that door were two people that had equal hate for them, but behind that door were the death seekers that made the ugly stain that will mark their wedding day for eternity.

"What the fuck are y'all doin'?" Sam whispered. "We're here to kill some muthafuckas, and the two of you start making out!" KC laughed as he watched the two of them continue to kiss.

"They always do dumb shit like this when we're going to handle business," KC explained. "I guess it's something about the danger that makes the both of them horny." Sam looked at him in disbelief and shook his head. He walked up to them and tapped JD on the shoulder.

"Y'all asses need to come the fuck on so we can get this shit out the way. We got shit to do, and it don't involve y'all playing kissy face!" Willow pulled away from JD and stared at Sam with a sarcastic smirk on her face.

"My bad, Pops," she replied. She looked over at JD with lust filled eyes then turned and started moving toward the door. She booted it in with one strong kick of her foot, and JD, Sam, and KC rushed inside with their weapons drawn. They stopped short when they saw that the couple were in the middle of having sex. Choppa climbed off of Danni and stared up at the arsenal of weapons pointed at them. Danni screamed once she noticed what was happening and quickly covered her body with the sheet.

"What the fuck!" Choppa shouted.

"We're about to step out the room while you and the Mrs. handle your business," said Sam, walking up to JD. "Y'all don't need our assistance, so ain't no sense in all of us being in here."

"This is true," JD replied with a smug smile on his face. "We'll be down in a second, and thanks for the backup."

"No problem, son," Sam replied. He hit JD on the back then signaled KC to follow him. KC took a few steps then stared at Danni for a second. A big grin spread across his face, and the words he spoke made Danni look at him in disbelief.

"I bet yo' ass wish you would have fucked me instead of JD now, bitch!" he laughed. "Yo' dumb ass couldn't leave well enough alone, and now, you about to be a dead bitch!" He walked out the room laughing, and Willow had a smile on her face while JD stared at both of them angrily. Danni noticed a slight bump emerging from Willow's belly by the way her vest was sticking out from the side view she had of her.

"Willow, is you pregnant?" Danni asked hesitantly.

"Why, yes, I am," Willow replied happily. "I'm also happily married to this wonderful man right here, but the two of you dumb muthafuckas tried to kill him on our wedding day, so now you're going to die tonight." Willow raised her gun and shot Danni twice in the head. Choppa looked over at Danni's lifeless body and noticed her brains splattered all over the headboard and on him. He nervously looked over at JD with fright in his eyes, and JD pulled the trigger, hitting Choppa in each and every place that he'd been shot in. Then, he stared vehemently into Choppa's eyes and unloaded the rest of his clips into Choppa's skull. He and Willow watched as his lifeless body fell from the bed on to the floor. JD looked over at Willow, and she returned his gaze with a satisfied look on her face.

"I love you, Lil' Baby," JD reminded her.

"I love you too, Big Baby," Willow replied.

"I told you not to call me that name in public," he replied, frowning.

"Those muthafuckas are dead, so they ain't trippin' off what I called you," Willow replied sarcastically. "Just give me a kiss, and let's go 'cause I'm horny as fuck! We can make a detour before we get on the highway and head to the Ozarks."

"Can you settle on a dick suck while we ride down the highway, and I'll dust you off at one of the rest stops?" JD asked jokingly. Willow lifted one of her guns in the air.

"Can I slap the shit out of you with this gun?" she asked sarcastically.

"Aye, you gone have to quit raisin' yo' pistol at me," said JD sternly. "That shit ain't cute, and you gon' respect me aaaannnd what I have to say whether you like it or not!" Willow lifted an eyebrow at him and put the gun down.

"You're absolutely right, husband, and I apologize," Willow replied humbly. She wrapped her arms around his neck and stared into his eyes. "The next time I raise a gun at you, I'm actually going to shoot you. That way we won't have any misunderstandings or miscommunication." JD continued to stare into Willow's eyes when he wrapped his arm around her waist and pulled her closer to him.

"Give me a kiss," he demanded. Willow smiled then pressed her lips firmly against JD's, letting his tongue journey into her mouth. They French kissed lustfully, not tripping off the fact that they were making out in the bloody room. All of their known enemies were dead, except Cypher, and he was going to make sure that he never crossed paths with Willow and JD ever again in life.

"Got damn!" Sam shouted. "Can the two of you come the fuck on so we can get out of here? You two muthafuckas are in here making out in front of some dead bodies!" JD pulled away from Willow and laughed at his father. Sam had told the couple that he was the one who killed O'Bannon the day before, and he even mentioned that he overheard the conversation that Willow had with O'Bannon before she left his hospital room. "Y'all always find the most fucked up time to be attached at the face!"

"So what, Pops!" Willow snapped. "Here we come! I don't know why yo' ass ain't just leave. You drove yourself, and your car is up the street." Sam glared at Willow with an eyebrow raised.

"JD, you hear how your wife is talking to your father?" asked Sam, sounding offended. JD looked at him nonchalantly.

"She talks to me like that, so what the fuck do you expect?" JD asked sarcastically. "C'mon, Lil' Baby. Let's get the fuck out of here. I'm suddenly feeling horny."

"Yay!" Willow cheered happily with a big grin on her face. "I'm glad you're seeing things my way!"

EPILOGUE

$\mathcal{J}$D and Willow made it down to the Ozarks safely. They decided to lay low for a while down there because it was off the radar and not too many people knew about it. JD still needed to heal from the wounds he'd sustained from being shot, and he just didn't feel safe right now due to his health not being at 100 percent. Willow didn't care where they stayed as long as she was with her man, and they found out that she was pregnant with a girl, which made her even happier. Willow was ecstatic, and surprisingly, so was JD. He figured a little girl would calm Willow's ass down, and she would discover what it's like to be a normal female. He loved the fire that his wife possessed inside, but he felt like it was time for her to calm the fuck down. They were happy with the way their life was shaping up to be, and their support system of family and friends would help them live a great life together.

Granny moved into a small three-bedroom house that JD had built behind the enormous million-dollar mansion he had constructed for Willow. He wanted to keep her close by, so moving her on their land was a no-brainer. Patsy helped by purchasing the plot of land, and she gave it to JD and Willow as a wedding gift. She wasn't in attendance at their nuptials, but she realized that Willow was never the problem in her marriage it was her husband. That's why when she got the insurance money for O'Bannon's death, she bought the property for her little cousin and apologized to both him and his wife when she presented it to them. She admitted her wrongdoing like a grown woman and wanted to use her gift as a peace offering to the couple. Also, she was about to start her new life with Ricky, and she wanted to have nothing but positive vibrations around her life from now on.

KC and Keena continued to hold the fort down while the parental front was away; aka JD and Willow. The couple wanted to do something nice for each one of their closest friends, so JD had Granny's house rehabbed and let Keena have it. He knew that the hoodrat wasn't going to leave the Ville, so now she had a permanent residence in that bitch, and it was all hers! Besides, she was closer to her new secret lover that had held her down when she got shot. KC stepped up and surprised Keena with how attentive he was to her, and she liked the attention. JD moved KC out of the apartment building and bought him the house next door to it. JD planned on rehabbing the apartments and moving tenants up in it. Yanni decided to stay with Yusuf in the Ozarks, so there was really no one to live in them. KC agreed to keep an eye out on them because JD and Willow agreed to keep one of the apartments for themselves. There was no way that JD was going to stop hustling right now, and Willow wasn't stupid enough to believe that he would. They would continue to go to school to get their degrees and open up the automotive business that JD promised Willow. It was just what they needed to get off all of the dope Locco had given them. Plus, the pipeline for that Cali bud had opened up to them, and it would be stupid for them to turn down such a good thing.

Charisma was arrested for his part in the kidnapping, burglary, and armed criminal action against Cypher at his house. Also, he faced corruption charges and a few other felonies in Virginia for his part in the robbery that occurred at the festival. Charisma's cousin, Ronnie, was being held on the same charges as Charisma, but he faced murder charges for the death of Indigo. Cypher agreed to testify against Ronnie, and he even asked that the death penalty be an option since Indigo was pregnant with his unborn child. The unsolicited publicity from the entire incident raised Cypher's popularity over the top, and the public mourned with him over the loss of his "fiancée" and "unborn child." Smile, it's the music industry. In the meantime, Cypher was licking his wounds from the loss of Willow. His depressed spirit helped him play the part he and Duke mapped out for his image. They came clean to each other about everything that had happened and decided to start over with a clean slate just like everyone else in this story. Duke was still creeping with Shaggy behind his wife's back, and Shaggy was still working for Cypher, but things were a lot different this time around. Cypher showed Shaggy more respect, and he treated Shaggy like an assistant instead of a flunky.

THE END

ACKNOWLEDGEMENTS

Thank you for coming along on this journey with me! This book was one of the challenges that I gave myself, and I'm happy with the turnout! JD and Willow were the embodiment of the love that two people could have for one another, and I hope you enjoyed this wild ride with them!

I would like to thank God for giving me this gift of writing. It is a blessing to be able to share my stories with you guys, and I appreciate each and every one of you that came along on my adventures! I would like to thank my publisher, Porscha Sterling, for believing in me and giving me the opportunity to put my thoughts out here in the world! I am truly grateful to you and the Royalty Publishing House Family for all of your love and support! I would like to give a special shout-out to Quiana Nicole for all of her help and support! I've come to understand that you are a major gear in this crazy machine that keeps us shining! And I want you to know that I appreciate you (XOXO)! I can't forget my AWESOME editor, Latisha Smith Burns, and her editing team at Touch of Class Publishing Services: "Where class meets perfection!" You are truly a gem, and I appreciate all of the love and support that you give me! You get my oddness, and I am so grateful that you do! To my test reader, LaShonda "Shawny" Jennings, thank you for your input and "realness!" You give me my reality check, and I appreciate the love and support!! Deanna Washington-Dean, thank you for keeping me on track with my timeline for putting out books. You keep me on schedule, and I appreciate it! LOL. Also, I would like to thank the ladies of Literary Plugs for their input and test reading over this body of work! You girls are Black Girl Magic! To my family and close friends, I ABSOLUTELY, POSITIVELY LOVE AND APPRECIATE EACH AND EVERY ONE OF YOU! Your support has been tremendous, and I am thankful that you are a part of my life! To my readers, THANK YOU! THANK YOU!! THANK YOU!!! YOU GUYS ARE ROCK STARS, AND I AM TRULY GRATEFUL TO YOU! YOU'RE THE REAL MVPS!

PEACE, LOVE, & BLESSINGS

Vivian Blue

CHECK ME OUT ON SOCIAL MEDIA

Facebook: Vivian Blue

Instagram: Authorvivianblue

Twitter: @VivBlueAuthor

My website: http://www.Vivianblueauthor.com

Amazon Author's Page: http://www.amzn.com/-/e/B0177JADR6

Facebook Likes Page:

http://www.Facebook.com/Vivian-Blue-3889021813110701

BOOK TITLES

Torn Between Two Bosses: The Series

*Rise of a Kingpin's Wife: The Series, with a follow up:
Forever A Kingpin's Wife: The Series*

A West Side Love Story: The Series

Gangsta: A Colombian Cartel Love Story: The Series

Friends Before Lovers, Standalone

Love, Marriage, and Infidelity: The Series

They Don't Know About Us: The Series *

War of the Hearts: The Series

*My Heart Is in Harmony by V. Marie
(young adult) Standalone*

Looking for a publishing home?

Royalty Publishing House, Where the Royals reside, is accepting submissions for writers in the urban fiction genre. If you're interested, submit the first 3-4 chapters with your synopsis to submissions@royaltypublishinghouse.com.

Check out our website for more information: www.royaltypublishinghouse.com.

Text ROYALTY to 42828 to join our mailing list!

To submit a manuscript for our review, email us at
submissions@royaltypublishinghouse.com

Text RPHCHRISTIAN to 22828 for our
CHRISTIAN ROMANCE novels!

Text RPHROMANCE to 22828 for our
INTERRACIAL ROMANCE novels!

Do You Like CELEBRITY GOSSIP?

Check Out QUEEN DYNASTY!
Visit Our Site: www.thequeendynasty.com

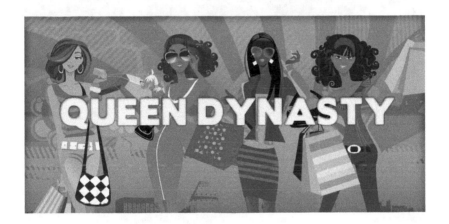

Get LiT!

Download the LiTeReader app today and enjoy exclusive content, free books, and more

CPSIA information can be obtained
at www.ICGtesting.com
Printed in the USA
LVHW02s1936030118
561663LV00015B/924/P